DIRTY
LITTLE
SECRETS

DIRTY
LITTLE
SECRETS

c. j. omololu

Walker & Company ✻ New York

For Bayo, who always knew

First published in the United States of America in February 2010 by
Walker Publishing Company, Inc., a division of Bloomsbury Publishing, Inc.
Paperback edition published in March 2011
www.bloomsburyteens.com

For information about permission to reproduce selections from this book, write to
Permissions, Walker BFYR, 175 Fifth Avenue, New York, New York 10010

The Library of Congress has cataloged the hardcover edition as follows:
Omololu, Cynthia Jaynes.
Dirty little secrets / by C. J. Omololu.
p.   cm.
Summary: When her unstable mother dies unexpectedly, sixteen-year-old Lucy must take control and find a way
to keep the long-held secret of her mother's compulsive hoarding from being revealed to friends, neighbors, and
especially the media.
ISBN 978-0-8027-8660-9 (hardcover)
[1. Secrets—Fiction. 2. Compulsive behavior—Fiction. 3. Mothers and daughters—Fiction.
4. Death—Fiction. 5. Self-reliance—Fiction. 6. High schools—Fiction. 7. Schools—Fiction.] I. Title.
PZ7.O54858Dir 2010   [Fic]—dc22   2009022461

ISBN 978-0-8027-2233-1 (paperback)

Book design by Nicole Gastonguay
Typeset by Westchester Book Composition
Printed and bound in the U.S.A. by Thomson-Shore Inc., Dexter, Michigan
10 9 8 7 6 5 4 3

All papers used by Bloomsbury Publishing, Inc., are natural, recyclable products
made from wood grown in well-managed forests. The manufacturing processes
conform to the environmental regulations of the country of origin.

DIRTY
LITTLE
SECRETS

chapter 1

before

Everyone has secrets. Some are just bigger and dirtier than others.

At least that's what I told myself whenever I stood in a crowd of normal-looking people and felt like I was the only one. The only person on the planet who had to hide practically everything that was real. It was soothing to look at all the unfamiliar faces and try to figure out the thing each person hid inside—true or not, it made me feel like less of a freak.

I'll bet that guy in the red hoodie picks his nose when he thinks nobody is looking. And the kid with the baseball cap pulled too low over his eyes? Totally stoned on the pain pills he steals from his mother. See how that girl in the corner stands just a little apart from everyone else? Her dad probably smacks her around when he's had too much to drink. Mom never laid a hand on me. There was that, anyway.

Despite the press of bodies, it was nice to know I could stand in the middle of a swirling mass of people and nobody would really see me. Nobody would know what my life was like, and nobody would ask me questions that were impossible to answer. I loved the glazed, faraway look people got as they glanced at you with a smile that faded as they quickly realized they didn't know you—their eyes scanned your face and, without a flicker of recognition, moved on to the next person. You were a factor in their life for a nanosecond and then you were gone.

Which is why being friends with Kaylie this year had been so stressful. With her, the nanosecond in art class had extended into months of hanging out, and there was always that nagging worry in the back of my head that it would turn out just like it had before. I always tried to be careful—watching what I said and what she knew, but sometimes it got exhausting. It was nice having a friend, though, nicer than I'd ever imagined, and that made it worth the effort.

As my eyes traveled over the people in the lobby, I couldn't help glancing in Josh's direction. Whether we were in the school hallway teeming with bodies or in a crowded movie theater lobby, my eyes went straight to him. Not that he had a clue or probably even remembered my name, but the last thing I wanted was for him to catch me staring. Which I wasn't. Much.

"Lucy, what do you want to see?" Kaylie was standing beside me, squinting up at the movie listings. She said that sticking her finger in her eye to put in contacts was gross and glasses made her look like a mathlete, so for now, she just wandered through life squinting at things. "The new one with Johnny Depp isn't out until next week, so it's either a chick flick with an unrealistically happy ending or an action/adventure with cute guys constantly in danger."

"You choose," I said, not wanting to make the wrong

decision and pick a movie she really wouldn't like. It was great that I'd finally found someone who shared my deep Johnny Depp love. Kaylie even had the complete set of 21 Jump Street DVDs, and we'd spent hours at her house devouring every episode—well, at least through season four when he left the show. Jump Street without Johnny was pointless. I fished around in my bag for my wallet. "I've got this one."

"Are you sure? I have money . . ."

"I'm sure," I said. "Dad sent me a fat check for Christmas. Technically, he's taking us to the movies." It wasn't like I was trying to buy Kaylie's friendship. At least I didn't mean it that way. It was just that sometimes I felt a little guilty. With everything I had to hide, the least I could do was pay for a movie now and then.

"Thanks," she said, putting her money back in her purse. "It's so cool he sends you cash. It would almost be worth having divorced parents if I could get paid regularly."

I grinned. "Not regularly, just sometimes when he's feeling particularly guilty. Like Christmas. Sort of his way of saying, "Thanks for NOT coming."

"What do you mean not coming—don't you ever visit him?"

I made a sound that might qualify as a snort if it was any louder. "Not if I can help it. His new wife, Tiffany, likes to think Dad never even dated before she came along, forget about the whole married-with-kids thing. She's only twenty-nine or something, and now that they have the baby, it's better that I don't exist in their reality."

"Ugh," Kaylie said. "She's twenty-nine? Isn't your sister that old?"

"Almost," I said. "Sara's going to be twenty-six in a couple of months."

"That," Kaylie said, making a face, "is gross. It's like he's doing his own daughter."

"Yeah," I agreed, smiling a little. It was nice to hear this stuff out loud and know it wasn't just me. "These days, he's nothing more than a sperm donor as far as I'm concerned."

"So that's why you hardly mention him?" She looked at me like she was waiting for more.

I scrambled for a good answer—it was stupid to have brought any of this up. Dad left when I was five, and he rarely looked back, so I tried not to care. Lately, all I saw of him was his pointy signature at the bottom of the checks I got every now and then, but talking about it always led to more questions, and you could never be too careful where the truth was involved. I tried to act casual, like I was concentrating on something on the opposite wall. "It's really no big deal," I said with a laugh that sounded fake even to me. "People get divorced all the time."

Kaylie shrugged. "Sometimes I bet my parents would like to pay me not to show up. That way they wouldn't have to stress over my grades all the time."

I relaxed into the safety of talking about something other than me. "No way. Your parents are totally cool. They just care if you get into a good school, is all." Her mom was like something out of one of those Nick at Nite sitcoms—their house was always so nice, and she didn't seem to mind that my sleeping bag was a permanent fixture on Kaylie's floor. I promised myself tonight was the last night I would stay over there for the rest of winter break. Hang out too long and people get tired of you.

Kaylie squinted up at the board again. "So, chick flick?"

"Sounds good." I gave the ticket info to the guy behind the little round window and handed him the cash.

Kaylie's little brother ran up and poked her in the shoulder. "I need five bucks."

"Mom gave you money, Daemon."

"That was for the movies," he said. "I need money for video games with the guys."

I took the tickets and my change from the cashier and stepped away from the window.

"Well, now you have a choice," Kaylie said. "You can either go to the movies like you're supposed to, or you can blow the money on loser video games and sit here for two hours until we're done."

Daemon frowned and looked back at the group of seventh-grade boys. I remembered how much it sucked to be the youngest and have to beg for everything. Sara and Phil were so much older than me that I always felt like I had extra parents instead of siblings. They were always talking about how they weren't given half as much stuff when they were kids and how Mom spoiled me just because I was the baby. Ever since they moved out, they seemed to have totally forgotten what it was like living there. "Here," I said, handing Daemon a couple of singles.

"Thanks," he yelled back as he raced toward his friends.

"You didn't have to do that," Kaylie said, glaring at him. "He's such a leech."

I shrugged, trying to play it off. The last thing I wanted was for her to think I wasn't on her side. "I'm loaded, remember?"

We still had fifteen minutes until the movie started, so I

tried to decide if I wanted to blow more money on an industrial-sized box of Milk Duds. They were such a rip-off here, but what was a movie without gobs of melted chocolate and caramel stuck to the roof of your mouth? Kaylie stood on her tiptoes beside me, looking for people she knew. She nudged me with her elbow. "He's totally staring at you."

"Who?" I asked, looking around. Somebody staring was generally not a good sign. Even worse if they were pointing.

She glanced over my shoulder and then back to me. "Like you don't know who. Josh Lee who. In the popcorn line."

As if I didn't already know where he was standing, or that he was wearing the blue jacket with the koi design he got at the beginning of the year. As if I didn't secretly watch him at lunch on the quad or practically lose my powers of speech every time our hands touched passing papers in physics.

"Right. I'm sure he's staring at you, not me." I pushed my hair out of my face and tried to look casually around. Kaylie was the one guys always stared at—tiny and cute, she could have been a cheerleader if she wanted to. Why she picked me to be her friend was still a mystery, but hanging out with her made my life seem almost normal.

She also never let a little thing like subtlety bother her. "Ooh, he's with Steve Romero! We should totally go over there and talk to them." She was a foot shorter than me but freakishly strong, pulling me in that direction before I could think up a good excuse not to go.

"No, Kaylie. Wait . . . ," I tried, but we were already there.

"Hey, Steve, hey, Josh," she said effortlessly. "What are you guys going to see?"

"That new Will Smith movie," Steve said, peering over the heads in front of him. "If this line ever gets moving."

"Oh, my God," she said, sounding surprised. "We are too." She bumped me with her hip and I managed a weak smile. I knew the smartest move I could make right then was to stand there and shut up.

"Hey," Josh said to me. He didn't look too annoyed and was even smiling a little.

"Hi," I managed, glancing up at those deep brown eyes. He had a certain Johnny Depp-ness that made my heart race and my cheeks burn. Somebody somewhere in his family must have been Asian—he had the deepest almond-shaped brown eyes. I was afraid to look at them too long in case they swallowed me up.

Josh had been in my eighth-grade English class when I'd first transferred in from Catholic school three years ago. He'd sat right in front of me, and I spent the entire semester staring at the back of his head, fighting with myself not to reach out and run my hand over the short, bristly hairs where they faded into his neck. He always smelled like soap and laundry detergent, and I leaned forward on my desk as often as I could to get a whiff of the light, clean scent. No matter how hard I tried, I could never smell like that.

"Poetry," Mr. Manillo had written on the board that first week. I groaned inside. I liked English well enough, but I absolutely hated poetry. Poets never said what they really meant, and your job was to spend hours trying to figure it out. In the end it usually wasn't worth the effort.

Mr. Manillo turned to face us as he spoke about the

mysteries of poetry. His eyes locked on mine and I quickly glanced down at my desk.

Too late. "Ms. Tompkins," he said. "You must have a favorite poet. I'm sure they gave you a good poetry foundation over at St. Ignatius."

Like most of the other teachers in this place, he either thought too highly of a Catholic school education, or he was making fun of me. I was never sure which it was.

"I don't . . . ," I started to say, but then noticed every eye in the room was on me. I knew my face was bright red and could feel droplets of sweat trickling down my back. I shifted uncomfortably in my seat, cleared my throat, and recited the only poem I had ever memorized.

Judging from the silence in the classroom, maybe a poem from third grade wasn't the best choice. Mr. Manillo cleared his throat. "That was, ah, interesting," he said. "And that piece was by . . ."

"Shel Silverstein," I said quickly. "*A Light in the Attic.*"

The whole class started laughing. And I knew right away they weren't laughing *with* me. I could hear other kids talking behind me. I glanced toward the open door, wishing the bell would ring so I could run out and be anonymous in the crowd. Instead, I stayed glued to my seat, staring straight ahead, my head pounding with embarrassment.

Mr. Manillo held up his hand. "People, please." He looked right through me. "This semester, we are studying the great masters of the seventeenth century and comparing the different forms of poetry. I'm afraid Mr. Silverstein is not on the syllabus."

The laughing started to subside as he called on Josh.

"Mr. Lee, do you have a better example of a popular poetry form?"

I was glad Josh was sitting in front of me so that I couldn't see the look of disgust that was probably on his face. At least he hadn't turned around to laugh directly at me. He cleared his throat and began to recite his poem in a clear, deep voice.

My pulse was pounding in my ears so loudly that at first I didn't listen, but then I began to hear people giggling all around the room and I started to pay attention. By the time he was done with "Jimmy Jet and His TV Set," I had the smallest but deepest grin on my face.

Mr. Manillo just stood in the front of the class with his arms crossed over his chest. "Is that meant to be amusing?"

"I'm sorry, Mr. Manillo, but Shel Silverstein rocks."

I didn't know why he'd done it, but he managed to get everyone to laugh *with* him and come off even cooler. He probably just felt bad for the new girl who didn't have a clue. If it were a movie, we'd have gotten together after class and discussed how much we had in common besides Shel Silverstein, and been bonded together from that very moment. Since this was only my real life, I just murmured "thanks" as I raced out of the room to change classes at the end of the period.

Josh was not just smart and gorgeous and apparently a Shel Silverstein fan, but he played guitar in a band called The Missing Peace and even wrote some of their songs. He'd also been one-half of the Cara-and-Josh super-couple since freshman year. At least until she got drunk and made out with someone else at that Halloween party a few months ago.

So now Josh was single and smiling at me, and I was standing right in front of him like a complete idiot with absolutely nothing to say. We stood in an uncomfortable silence, staring at the snack bar menu board, as Kaylie inched imperceptibly closer to Steve so she could put her hand on his arm for emphasis as she spoke. She made it look so easy.

"Maybe we should leave them alone," Josh joked, nodding at Steve and Kaylie, whose heads were now bent deep in conversation.

"Yeah," I said, mentally beating myself up for such a lame answer. I turned phrases over in my head, trying to come up with something casual and clever. *So what's your favorite Shel Silverstein poem these days?* Right. He'd never remember something that happened so long ago. *Where's the band playing next?* Too groupie slut. *Did you know our children would be gorgeous?*

I felt a hard tap on my shoulder. "Excuse me?" a girl's voice demanded.

I turned to see Justine Hildebrandt, Cara's best friend, standing with her hands on her hips. "The end of the line is back there, in case you didn't know."

"Oh, we weren't—," I started to say, but Justine cut me off, indignation flashing in her eyes. She glanced at Josh with a lot more anger than the situation called for, but continued to talk to me. All of a sudden, I had a pretty good idea what her secret was.

"Right. We saw you two cut in front of us," she said. "Don't think we didn't." A group of JV cheerleaders stood with her, nodding their heads in unison. At least Cara Lassen and her perfect highlights were nowhere in sight.

"No, really," I managed. "Kaylie just wanted to say hi." I reached out to grab Kaylie's arm, but she was so blissed out talking to Steve she didn't even notice we were about to be ambushed by the entire Gompers High School cheerleading squad.

"Ease up, Justine," Josh said to her. "I've been saving Lucy's place." He smiled at me. "What took you so long?"

"Um," I squeaked, startled by the fact that he'd actually said my name out loud.

Josh reached over and put his arm around my shoulders, and it was everything I could do not to gasp. Nobody had touched me for such a long time that just a little bit of contact made my knees wobbly. I tried to savor the weight of his arm on the back of my neck, the faint, warm, clean smell making me want to turn and bury my face in his collar. My heart was beating so fast I was sure he would notice the jolt of energy that ran up my spine. I should have stopped time then—framed this one perfect moment so I could go back and look at it again and again. His shiny brown hair flopped in his eyes as he gave me a barely perceptible wink.

Justine leaned back and crossed her arms in front of her chest. "You're here with *her?*" I didn't blame her for not believing him. *I* could hardly believe I was standing in front of a bunch of cheerleaders with Josh Lee's arm casually draped around my shoulders.

Josh pulled me closer to him, and I could feel the heat from his body and the muscles in his arm as he flexed. "Of course," he said, like it was the most natural thing in the world. I knew it was all a joke—he was only doing it so Justine would turn around and tell Cara. Josh probably wanted to get back together with her, and sparking some jealousy was always a good choice. Still, if I was being used, I can't say I minded all that much.

"What can I get you?" the old guy behind the counter asked as we reached the front of the line. Josh dropped his arm and my shoulders felt neglected and cold immediately.

"One jumbo popcorn," he said, turning his back on Justine and the other girls. "You don't mind sharing, do you?" he asked, bumping my arm. I smiled and shook my head, prepared to go along with the joke as long as he wanted. Not only did I get to pretend to be with Josh, but I got to piss off Justine Hildebrandt, and that was never a bad thing. As we walked toward the theater, I couldn't help but glance back at Justine and feel a secret thrill at the scowl on her face as Josh pretended to be interested in walking with me.

I didn't even really like popcorn, but I ate it through the whole movie because our fingers brushed as we reached into the bucket at the same time. I was glad the movie was blaring so I didn't have to think of anything interesting to say and could just pretend we were on an actual date instead of playing some game that would end as soon as the lights came on.

Steve and Kaylie weren't exactly holding hands as they walked out of the theater, but their shoulders kept brushing as they bumped into each other. Cozy, for sure. I was walking behind them as slowly as I could to make the moment last as long as possible. Pretty soon, we'd reach the big glass front doors, and that's where it would stop. Without Justine around, Josh wouldn't have to pretend anymore, and I'd be just me, stuck watching him safely from a distance once again. We'd almost crossed the lobby in complete silence when Josh stopped and turned to me. "Listen, I play guitar in a band with a bunch of other guys. We're not too bad—mostly covers, but I write some songs too."

He said this like I knew nothing about him. Like I didn't lie in bed in the dark some nights and picture him saying something just like that. I held my breath, hardly believing it was really happening, partly hoping it wasn't. It was the perfect guy saying the perfect thing at the perfectly wrong time. "Anyway," he continued, "we're playing at a party tomorrow night down on Marina. If you're not doing anything, you want to come by?"

Maybe it was the bright lights of the lobby after being in the dark theater, but the whole place seemed to start throbbing. "That would be cool," I managed. I had to look down at the ground in order to actually say what had to come next. "But I, uh, don't think I can make it." Every fiber of my being was screaming "yes," but I knew I couldn't go. Pretending I was on a date with Josh Lee was one thing. Meeting him somewhere on purpose was another. Getting close to someone like him would just be way too risky.

He actually looked a little bummed, which made my heart skip. Either he was a better actor than I thought or this wasn't completely a joke. "Got a date with someone else?" he asked, watching me out of the corner of his eye.

"Ha! No," I said a little too quickly. "I mean, no. But . . ." God, I'd wished for this moment to happen since I first laid eyes on him, and now that he was asking me out, I was racking my brain for a good reason why I couldn't go.

He must have seen my indecision. "We play pretty early if you have to be home." He reached out with his pinky and curled it around mine, playful but secure. I stared at the spot where we touched, hardly able to believe any of this was real.

I looked into those big brown eyes, and against everything

I knew I should do, I heard myself say, "Okay. I . . . I think I can make it." It was going to be fine, I reasoned. Dating Josh Lee for real would be impossible. Hanging out one single night might be doable.

Josh grinned and squeezed my hand for the briefest second. "I can pick you up if you want."

And there it was already. My whole body stiffened at the thought. I had to keep him away from the house no matter what. "Oh, no. That's okay." I tried to sound as casual as possible. "I'll come with Kaylie. I'll probably stay over at her house, anyway." So much for no more sleepovers. I was sure Steve would be at the party too, which meant she'd be into it.

"Easier to tell your mom you're at Kaylie's than you're out at a party?"

I swallowed hard. "Something like that. She's, um, really religious and doesn't let me go out much."

Josh nodded like he understood. "Must be rough."

"Yeah. Sometimes it is." I nodded slowly and looked down at the floor so I couldn't see his face.

That was the trouble with secrets—the lies you had to tell to keep them hidden almost made you feel worse than telling the truth.

Almost.

chapter 2

9:00 a.m.

After spending all night at Kaylie's going over every detail, I stood at the bottom of our cracked cement walkway the next morning, the ache in my stomach starting the minute I saw Mom's car in the driveway. She must have switched schedules with someone at work again. Just when I'd counted on her to be gone.

I really wanted to be alone to think about the party tonight—get it sorted in my head so I wouldn't make any big mistakes, but if Mom was home, the hassling would start the minute I hit the front door. Kaylie was excited about the whole Steve and Josh double-dating angle and was going to spend the day figuring out what we were going to wear. It was hard not to get caught up in the excitement. Josh had asked me to come to a party. Me. To a party. Where his band was playing. Unbelievable.

Kaylie's mom didn't have to be to work until late, so she'd given me a ride home on the way. Like always, I waited until she had driven around the corner and was safely out of sight before I headed for the front door. Our little gray and white house really didn't look that bad from out here. If you were paying attention, you could spot the black mold gathering along the edges of the living room windows and the way the curtains were pressed against the glass by stacks of boxes. Those were just small hints about what was really behind the shingled walls, but nobody on the outside ever noticed.

I kicked at the tufts of grass as I slowly made my way toward the porch. Even though Mom had to park the car in the driveway because of all the junk that filled the garage, from out here the house looked pretty normal.

All of our secrets started at the front door.

The TV was on too loud, as always, mercifully covering any noise I made as I came in. Standing on my tiptoes, I peeked into the living room over the tops of the newspaper piles and bags of junk that flooded every inch of open space in the house. Mom wasn't in her usual spot in the vomit-green recliner, and the lady on television was trying to sell genuine synthetic sapphires to nobody. I let myself relax a little—maybe I could make it to the safety of my room without another confrontation.

Hurrying past the kitchen and down the hall, I glanced around the narrow pathways we'd carved in the piles of news-papers and garbage over the years. It had gotten easier to get around since I'd grown tall enough to see over the top of a lot of it. Mom was only about five-foot six and she didn't stack things higher than she could reach. When I was smaller, I used to pretend I was walking at the bottom of the Grand Canyon with the cliffs rising over my head, only instead of a steel blue sky with puffy white clouds, there was a cracked plaster ceiling and a burned-out lightbulb.

At the bend in the hallway, a tall pile of *National Geographics* had fallen over and blocked the narrow pathway that led to her room. *That's really going to make her mad,* I thought as I turned and walked toward my room. Mom didn't go into her room much anymore, but I wondered why she hadn't straightened up the pile right away. Even with all this stuff crammed into the house, having things out of place made her even crazier. Especially if she thought I'd had something to do with it.

That's what last night's argument had been about. As usual.

I'd been throwing clothes in my backpack to go to Kaylie's when I heard her shouting from the living room, "Lucy!"

I pretended not to hear her until she called for a third time, then I pushed my door open and yelled down the hall, "What?"

She squeezed past the piles of newspapers and overflowing plastic bags in the hallway until she could see me. Her red hair showed an inch of gray at the roots, and wiry strands of it were hanging in front of her face. She put her hands on her hips, and I watched her ropy veins wiggle and move underneath her chapped, red skin. "What did you do with them?"

I shut my eyes and slowly opened them again. Here we go. "With what?" I asked, keeping my voice as even as possible. Any hint of sarcasm would send her over the edge, and I really, really wanted to go out tonight.

"You know what. My good scissors. The ones with the black handles."

"I haven't seen your scissors, Mom," I said, allowing just a hint of a sigh to creep into my voice as I tried to duck back into my room.

"Lucy Tompkins! You never put anything back where you found it. I need those scissors and I can't find them anywhere." She leaned forward and tried to peer over my shoulder and into my room. I quickly stepped into the hallway and tried to block her view, although I knew she'd be in there looking through my stuff within seconds of my leaving.

Her eyes began to fill with tears. "I need them right now. There's an article on dog training I wanted to clip for your sister, and I always keep my good scissors on the table right next to the chair. Now they're missing and I know you took them."

In a voice you'd usually use on a three-year-old I said, "Honestly, I didn't do anything with them." For once, this was the truth. I hadn't touched her stupid scissors. "Kaylie's coming to pick me up in a couple of minutes, so I have to finish here."

The tears were starting to spill over her eyelids and run unchecked down her cheeks. "After sixteen years, this is what I get? No help at all? You're just going to run off with your *friends* and leave me here alone? Can't you spare two minutes to help me look?"

I backed into my room and left her standing in the hallway looking old and defeated. God, I couldn't wait to get out of here and get my own place. I'd live all by myself and not answer to anybody. Less than two years—I just had to keep telling myself, less than two years and I could leave this all behind like Phil and Sara had.

I finished packing, but a lump of guilt settled into my chest. I listened to her shuffling around in the living room until I couldn't stand it anymore. In a few minutes, I'd be out of here, hanging out with Kaylie at the movies, but I knew she'd spend the next twelve hours sitting on the recliner watching TV by herself, which despite everything made me feel kind of bad.

Lifting my backpack onto my shoulders, I checked the time. Kaylie wouldn't be here for a few more minutes, and it would make Mom happy if I at least made an effort. It's not like I had a prayer of finding her stupid scissors in the avalanche of garbage, but I could fake it. At some point, I'd just started to go along with her and pretended everything was normal and this was the way everyone lived. It was easier that way.

I squeezed through the hallway and spotted Mom sorting through a stack of pictures in the living room. "Did you find them?" I asked hopefully.

She looked up from the pictures like she'd forgotten I was in the house. A frown settled on her face as she refocused her anger on me. "How could *I* find them when I have no idea what *you* did with them?"

I looked around the room, trying to concentrate on all the horizontal surfaces where a pair of scissors could be set down and never seen again, like some crazy picture from one of those *I Spy* books. I inched my way over to the recliner. "I think I might have put them back over here," I said, as cheerfully as I could manage. I picked up a plastic bag from the drugstore and looked inside.

Mom leaned over and snatched the bag from my hands. "Don't touch that," she said. "I need those things for work."

It always came down to trying to find the right answer in a game where I didn't know any of the rules. If I didn't help look for the thing *I* supposedly lost, she'd be mad. If I touched any of *her* stuff, she'd be mad. It was just a question of what was going to make her less mad at any given moment. The exhaustion I always felt in these situations began creeping into my bones. "Okay," I said in my most patient voice. "I'm going to retrace my steps back to the dining room."

As I tried to turn in the narrow pathway, my backpack clipped the corner of a box that was stacked on top of some newspapers. It wobbled and started to fall, but I caught it in time and eased it back.

"Watch out!" Mom yelled. "I swear, you are such a klutz! Can't you even walk through a room without sending half the contents to the floor?"

No matter how many times she said stuff like that, it still settled heavily onto my chest. I dug my fingernails into the palms of my hands, hoping the pain would distract me from crying. "Sorry," I mumbled.

Mom shook her head and sighed, as if the world's problems had been placed on her shoulders. "That's the best you can do? Always knocking everything over, losing my things. You never lift a finger—"

She was just warming up when Kaylie's signature two short beeps followed by one long beep sounded out front. It was like the cavalry had come to rescue me from hell.

"I have to go," I said. I pulled my backpack tight against my shoulders and inched carefully along the path toward the front door. The relief I always felt when I stepped out of the house was like plunging into a cold pool on a hundred-degree day.

"I hope you have a *lovely* time," Mom said, turning back to the pile of photos, the saga of the lost scissors temporarily forgotten. I said nothing, but shut the door just a little more forcefully than was necessary as I left, hopefully dislodging a pile or two to give her something to do for the night.

Now, as I stood in front of my bedroom door the next morning, I wondered if she'd ever found those stupid scissors. I pushed it open and stepped inside, leaving the rest of the house behind me. Compared to everywhere else in this place, my room was like paradise, with surfaces that weren't covered with bags of useless garbage, and with a bed you could actually sleep in.

The first time I'd really cleaned my room a couple of years ago, she'd totally freaked. I'd been babysitting at the Callans' when I got the idea to clean my room. I wanted my bedroom to look the same as the ones their kids had—carpet on the floor you could see and a desk you could reach without having to wade through drifts of crap. A room that could be dusted on occasion because there wasn't so much clutter, with a bed that didn't have to be cleared to be slept in. It's not like anyone else would see it, but still it would be nice. I'd started one morning when Mom was at work, and by the time she got home you could really see the difference. Despite my better judgment, I thought she might be happy about it, might be glad that for once I'd done some work around here. I couldn't have been more wrong.

The whole neighborhood could hear her ranting out by the garbage cans as she dug through them for the dirty stuffed animals, clothes that were too small, games with missing pieces, and everything else I had thrown out. I got the usual lecture about starving people in Africa who didn't have anything nice at all as she marched the garbage bags back into my room.

Not that I could ever figure out what a starving African child would do with a one-eyed Care Bear. After she'd fallen asleep in the recliner, I'd taken the bags back out of my room and shoved them deep into the dining room where they quickly got absorbed into the mess and disappeared. From then on, I cleaned my room by relocating the junk to other parts of the house.

Soon after that first time, she made Phil take my door off the hinges and put it in the garage so she could keep an eye on me. At least that's what she said. Phil never said anything, but I could tell he felt bad about it. He was a senior in high school by then and did whatever it took to get by—just marking time until he could move out and be on his own like Sara had done years before.

You'd think a person would get used to being completely exposed, but I never did. I always slept facing the wall, but it still felt like someone was watching me. It took almost a year of careful negotiation to get the door put back on, minus the lock and doorknob so it didn't actually close all the way, but I wasn't about to complain. Apparently, nobody as sneaky and selfish as me deserved any privacy—you never knew what I might get up to in here if I had an actual door that locked. I might go crazy and vacuum the carpet or, worse, wash the windows. Anytime I cleaned something, she took it as a personal attack, like I was saying she wasn't good enough to do it herself. Which, in reality, she wasn't.

I reached into my jacket pocket for the ticket stub from the movies last night and smiled to myself. Smoothing over the corner that had gotten bent, I could almost feel the weight of Josh's arm around my shoulders. I put the stub carefully in my vintage Partridge Family lunchbox. A calm feeling came over me as I sifted through the tickets I kept there—movies, the baseball game with Dad when I went out to see him that one summer, Disney on Ice when I was seven, and the circus from before Mom decided it was cruelty toward animals and we stopped going.

My room was freezing, so I reached down and clicked on the ancient space heater. One hard smack to the side got it running again, the orange glow from the coil inside making me feel warmer even before the heat actually kicked in.

I wasn't sure when the furnace had broken completely, but it hadn't worked right since last year. I'd have to call Phil and have him come try to fix it again. He hated having to come home from college to deal with the house, but we didn't really have a choice. The last repairman didn't get past the front hallway before realizing the place was too full of crap to even get near the hot water heater. He threatened to report Mom to Child Protective Services if she didn't clean it up. He must not have, because CPS never showed up. Neither did another repairman. Mom said a lot of people in the old days had no hot water or indoor heat, and it didn't hurt them any.

Because she had an early dentist appointment, I hadn't had time to take a shower at Kaylie's this morning. I took inventory in my bathroom mirror to see how bad things were getting. Cutting my hair short had been a great idea, because it made showerless days not as noticeable. I could probably hit the gym for a shower later today so I'd look as good as possible for tonight—the mere thought of Josh sent an electric thrill through my entire body. Maybe I'd even manage to get a workout in this time, and justify Dad paying for the membership. Although from the looks of my hamper, a trip to the laundromat this afternoon was probably more important.

I was heating up some water in my microwave to wash my face when the doorbell rang. I froze like we always did, hoping whoever was out there wouldn't hear anyone moving around inside. The doorbell rang again a few seconds later, and I could hear distant knocking. Unless she knew who it was, Mom wouldn't get it, either, so we'd both just wait until they got tired and went away. Except whoever it was wasn't going away. After it rang insistently a third time, I quietly opened my door and tiptoed down the hall.

There was a spot in the dining room where you could look out the window without anyone seeing. Just as I reached it, I heard a car pull away from the front of the house and exhaled the breath I hadn't realized I was holding. Having someone at the front door always tied my stomach up in knots.

As I walked back to my room, I wondered why Mom didn't open her door even a crack. Usually she at least listened to see if she could figure out who it was. She must be sick or something if she didn't bother to come out at all. Her room was so full of stuff that she hardly ever slept in there anymore, but she occasionally shoved everything off the bed if she really needed to use it.

Feeling like I should at least make sure she was okay, I headed toward her room. The *National Geographics* blocked a good six feet of the hallway, and I'd slowly started to pick my way over the mountain of fallen magazines when I saw it. One of Mom's slippers sticking out from under the pile.

"Mom?" I bent down and threw some of the magazines off until I had uncovered her leg. I shook it. "Mom?" It didn't jiggle like it normally would; it just felt solid and heavy. "Mom!"

Because the paths we'd carved through all the garbage over the years were only wide enough to accommodate one relatively skinny person, I had to kneel down by her foot and stretch out on my hands so I could reach her face. I frantically tossed magazines to the side until her head was completely uncovered. Her eyes were closed and her mouth had a purplish tinge around the edges. I followed her outstretched arm and saw her inhaler just out of reach on the ground. She must have been having an asthma attack when she fell, pulling a decade's worth of magazines with her as she went.

"Mom!" I reached up to shake her shoulder, but only felt the heaviness of her body as it refused to move. "Mom!" I yelled a little louder. "Come on!" *This was not happening. This was not happening right now.* My heart was pounding so loud it sounded like the ocean in my ears.

I reached up and with a quick motion put my index finger out to feel her face. Her cheek was mottled and cold. Even though she was pale, my finger made a faint mark on her skin where I'd touched her. I scrambled backward, slipping on the magazines, and slammed into a pile of newspapers, sending them cascading down on us both. My breath was quick and short as I tossed them off me, throwing them as far as I could down the hallway until I could struggle to my feet.

Standing alone in the cold, dark hallway, I felt my teeth start to chatter, and I couldn't keep my hands from shaking. "This can't be real. This can't be real," I repeated over and over as I crouched down, pulling the newspapers off her, revealing her face one more time.

Maybe I was wrong. Maybe she was just out cold. I grabbed her shoulders and shook them so hard her head flopped from side to side. "Get up! Come on, Mom, *please*, this is not funny. Get up!" If wishing really worked, she would have jumped up and scared the crap out of me right then—that would teach me to leave her and try to get on with my own life. It would have been the best trick ever, except practical jokes weren't her style.

I dropped her shoulders back to the floor and crumpled down beside her as I realized nothing I could do was going to make any difference. This was not the way things were supposed to go. I sat, leaning carefully on the stack of newspapers behind me, trying to pull rational ideas through the swarm of thoughts running through my head.

What if the stack of magazines had fallen when I'd slammed the door last night? She was in the living room when I left, but what if they'd moved just enough to send them crashing down as she walked by? All she had to do was clip the corner of one, and the whole thing could have come down right on top of her. I wondered how long she had been lying there, her inhaler just out of reach, her breathing getting shallow and more ragged. Did she know what was happening? A chill went through me as I pictured her trapped and weak, calling my name as her voice got quieter and quieter. I could almost hear the echo of her cries in the hallway.

I stood up to try to shake off the heavy feelings that were settling inside. As I looked at her unmoving body, I knew deep down Mom wasn't sick and she wasn't messing around. She was really and truly dead.

chapter 3

10:00 a.m.

I pulled the phone from my pocket, my throat feeling so thick I wasn't sure I'd be able to speak. *This was not happening.* I should have stayed home last night. Mom's asthma was getting bad, and she always needed her inhaler when she got upset. Those stupid scissors. If I'd only taken two minutes to help her find them, everything would be okay right now.

The phone's display shone brightly as I opened it to dial 911, the numbers blurring through the tears that had started to form in my eyes. I blinked hard. My fingers hovered over the first number as I looked down the hall at the piles of magazines, newspapers, clothes, plastic bags, and boxes of her stuff that choked all but a few narrow, winding paths through the house. I knew it smelled like rotting garbage in here, remembered it in one of the recesses of my brain. It was the same smell of decay I always worried would follow me out of the house, clinging to my clothes like a sock to Velcro. I'd lived with it for so long, I didn't even notice the smell anymore.

But the paramedics would.

They'd definitely notice the stink, the decay, and the sea of garbage that cascaded from the center of every room and built up along the walls like rolling waves. I looked back along the path that snaked through the hall and then took a sharp turn into the dining room. The only way through the house was along these ant tracks, and they were much too narrow for any type of stretcher to get through. It would probably take the paramedics hours just to clear out a path wide enough to get her out of here. And what if it wasn't just them?

My mind started racing and my heart beat faster as I realized what could happen. As soon as the paramedics showed up, the news cameras would probably follow—big cameras with bright lights on top so they could illuminate the dark pathways. Newspeople had radios and sat listening to the paramedic and police reports just waiting for a story like this. I could see the teasers now—"Local Woman Dies Surrounded by Filth and Squalor—tune in at eleven." Our house would be the spotlight report on all the networks, maybe even on some of those morning shows. I'd seen a story on the news one time about this lady who died in a trailer full of garbage. They videotaped the mess, and the perfectly overhairsprayed news anchors shook their heads at how anyone could live like that. They didn't come out and say it, but I knew what they were all thinking: she was a freak. Who else would possibly live their entire lives surrounded by garbage? Freaks.

They'd probably want to interview me, and find out how we lived like this for so long—and because the evidence was right there in front of their faces, I'd have to tell them. About all of it. Kaylie would see it, and that would be the last time I'd stay over at her house. She'd be so disgusted by how we lived for all these years, she'd wonder how we could have ever been friends. That's what had happened the last time a friend had come over, and the house hadn't been nearly this bad then. I thought of the look in Josh's eyes when he asked me to the party, and knew I'd never see that look again. I wouldn't be able to stay here after that. I'd have to move away and change schools one more time, starting all over when I just had a lousy year and a half until graduation. Where would I even go?

I braced myself against a pile of newspapers and slid to the floor. My chest was hollow, and I'd never felt so lonely in my life. None of this was normal. If Kaylie had found her mom lying dead on the floor, she'd be bawling her eyes out. Somewhere deep down, I was pretty sure I loved Mom—the mom who used to push all the kids on the swings at school when it was her turn to do yard duty. The mom who actually hugged me as I left in the morning and stopped by my room to say good night. I could cry for that mom. I wasn't sure how I felt about this mom.

At that moment the kitchen phone rang, the sound ricocheting around the still house, and I jumped, my heart beating almost visibly in my chest. Before I could think about what to say, I ran to get it just to make the noise stop.

"Hello?" It came out as more of a croak, so I cleared my throat and tried again. "Hello?"

"Joanna?" I wasn't sure if I was relieved it was only Nadine, Mom's supervisor at work.

"Oh, hi. No, it's Lucy."

"Are you okay, dear? You sound like you're breathing hard."

As much as I knew that I should, I couldn't tell her what

had happened. For now, that fact had to be another part of our secret. Once I told someone, I wouldn't be able to take it back. "I, um . . . yeah, I'm fine. I was just racing for the phone. From the backyard."

"Sorry about that, darlin'," she said. "I'm looking for your mama. Her shift started at seven, but she hasn't been in or called or anything, and that is just not like her. I came by the house a little bit ago on my break, but nobody answered the door."

I glanced down the hallway toward the fallen pile of cheerful yellow magazines.

"Right," I said. "I've been outside doing some stuff in the backyard, and I must have missed you. Mom asked me to call you, but I forgot. She's, uh, got some sort of flu and probably won't be in for a few days." Mom was an oncology nurse, and the last thing they wanted was sick people down at the hospital.

"Oh dear," she said. "Is there anything I can do?"

I thought about Mom where I'd left her lying all alone. "No," I said. "Not really."

"Chicken soup? Advil? I can stop by on my way home," she said.

"Really," I said, "we're fine. I've got it under control."

"Your mom is blessed to have you," she said. "I don't know what she's going to do without you when you go off to college, especially now that everyone else is gone. It's always hardest when the baby leaves."

"I'm sure she'll manage," I said, wondering how blessed she'd think Mom was if she could see us now. I tried to tune into the conversation, but my eyes were scanning the tops of the debris piles that clogged the kitchen and the dining room. The smell was so bad in the kitchen I stretched the cord as far as I could into the dining room so I wouldn't have to breathe it in. Even in here, the visual noise from the garbage made it difficult to see the individual pieces that made up the mountain. A plastic bag from the grocery store full of God knows what. A stack of old margarine tubs. A box full of empty egg cartons and toilet-paper tubes. A pile of clothes still on their wire hangers from some adventure to the dry cleaners years ago. And green plastic storage bins stacked so high they brushed the ceiling in every room. Green plastic bins were like crack for Mom— she couldn't get enough of them.

"Lucy, honey?"

"I'm sorry." I shook my head trying to pick up the last threads of the conversation. "You cut out on me there for a second."

"I was asking you if you'd picked a college yet. Don't you have to start applying soon?"

"Oh, yeah," I said. "Well, really, we have a whole year before things are due. They don't make you decide until senior year."

"Well, you be sure to come down here soon for a visit. You haven't been in here to see us for such a long time."

"I will," I said. "Soon. Oh, listen, I hear her calling me. I really have to go."

"Okay, doll," Nadine said. "You tell your mama just to take it easy and not worry about us. She works so hard, I'm sure she needs the rest. You holler if you need anything."

"Thanks. I will."

I leaned into the kitchen to put the handset back and wiped

it with the sleeve of my jacket. We still had one of those big, square, wall-mounted phones everyone else got rid of years ago. A while back, Mom had bought one of those fancy digital systems with four portable handsets and an answering machine. It was good in theory, but it took less than a week for every last handset to be lost in the piles, and eventually I dug out this old mustard yellow phone and put it back on the wall. Ugly, but at least we always knew where it was.

Just talking to someone on the outside had calmed me down a little. My breathing got back to normal, and I felt like I could think straight again. Nadine thought we were fine. People all over town were doing regular things at work, spending winter break at the mall, going to the grocery store. Nobody knew. I had time.

Everybody still thought we were exactly like them—I just had to keep it that way.

I took a couple of deep breaths and looked down at the cell phone that was still in my left hand. Once I dialed those three numbers, there would be no turning back. Slowly, I closed it. There really wasn't much reason to hurry, if you thought about it. Why call 911 when someone was so obviously dead? The paramedics couldn't help someone who'd had their head cut off or had been shot straight through the heart—or had died under a six-foot-tall stack of *National Geographics*.

I walked back toward Mom's room, forcing my eyes to travel past the magazines and focus on Mom's face. She looked peaceful—relaxed, even. If you didn't know she was dead, she actually looked pretty good. Most of the time lately her face had rippled with frown lines. At least when I was around.

I couldn't even remember the last thing I said to her. Last

words were supposed to be meaningful, about how much you loved the person and how much you were going to miss them, and the last thing she'd said to me was something about scissors. Or was it about going to Kaylie's? Of course, she probably had other last words that nobody was around to hear. Did those count? My mind started reeling again, and I shook my arms to try to release some of the energy.

I took a couple of steps backward toward my room so I could think a little better. Here, the path was wider and you could see patches of the dirty brown carpet that covered all the floors, but only appeared here and there through the drifts of garbage, like jagged cracks in the earth. My chest felt heavy, and my breathing was fast and shallow as the panic started to wash over me again. I couldn't possibly deal with all of this by myself.

I clicked my phone open again. This was crazy. I hit the numbers and held it to my ear, my left hand shaking so violently I had to reach over with my right hand to try to steady it. It rang twice. Three times. *Come on, answer*, I thought, all of a sudden feeling like I had to hurry. I switched the phone to my other ear just in time to hear the voice mail click on.

Hey, this is Phil. I'm probably on the phone, so leave a message and I'll call you back. I waited for the beep, and then snapped the phone shut. What kind of message could I possibly leave him?

Hey, Phil, it's Lucy. Mom's dead, and if you don't get over here and help me quick, everyone's gonna know our secret, and life as you know it will be over. Phil had just as much to lose as any of us—a serious girlfriend, fraternity brothers, a fancy job as soon as he graduated. I tapped the phone against my forehead, trying to think. What did I want him to do, anyway? He couldn't make her less dead. At least he could be here to help me decide. I only knew calling 911 was as good as ruining all of our lives.

From where I was standing in the hallway, I couldn't see Mom's head anymore, only her legs and feet. It looked like she was still wearing her robe, and she had on those nasty slippers like she always did when she was home. Mom had worn the same brown suede slippers as long as I could remember—repairing rips with silver duct tape until that wore through as well and left dirty, sticky marks from the adhesive.

I closed my eyes and tried to think of nothing. Just for a few minutes, if I could get my mind clear, my thoughts could sort themselves out, and I would know what to do and how to feel. It was just the shock of it all that had me confused.

Past the kitchen, I squeezed myself into the living room and turned off the TV so I could think without it squawking around inside my head. We only had one trash can in the whole house so Mom could monitor what went in it. If something couldn't be recycled, it could be reused. If it couldn't be reused, it could be composted. If it couldn't be recycled, reused, or composted, it could be put in a pile somewhere in this house where it would never again see the light of day.

I could put a few bags out in the trash bin, but then what? A few bags in the garbage wouldn't begin to make a dent in the accumulation of almost an entire lifetime of "treasures." Which was mostly what other people called trash.

I walked back into the kitchen and took a look around. I hadn't looked in here for a long time—with good reason. The microwave and minifridge in my room were all I ever needed, so I avoided this part of the house at all costs. The counters were stacked with dirty dishes, petrified pizza boxes, and take-out containers full of food that had sat long enough to congeal into one black, furry mass. I knew the stove was to the left of the sink, but I couldn't see it beyond the one clear spot right in the middle of the room. The cupboard under the sink was open, and the big pipe underneath drained into an old green bucket that sat on the floor half full of moldy water. Back when we still used the sink, I had rigged this so the waste emptied into the bucket, and we could take the bucket and dump it outside. The system was so primitive it almost made me smile—I could do a lot better now.

The sink itself was full of a uniform dark brown mass that could have been anything once. It looked like chocolate pudding, but I could guarantee it wasn't.

As I glanced around at the remains of the kitchen, I could feel trickles of sweat running down my neck despite the frigid house. I couldn't fix this. It had taken years to get it this bad; how was I supposed to fix it overnight?

I wrapped my jacket tighter around me and wished for more time. A few days—a week, maybe, and I could have this place looking okay enough to let people in. It's not like I had to make it perfect, just good enough so it wasn't a freak show.

A draft of cold air came from somewhere and brushed against my cheek. It was so cold inside, I could see my breath hang in front of me. It felt almost colder in here than it did outside, and, without the furnace working, this whole place was turning into one giant freezer. I'd have to keep moving or I'd freeze to death along with her.

Oh my God—my stomach did a flip-flop as the idea started to form. It was *freezing* in here!

A glimmer of hope started flickering inside me as I picked my way to the other side of the room as fast as I could, my thoughts racing one step ahead. This was totally crazy and totally wrong and totally the only hope I had at all.

The smell near the sink was so bad I had to hold my breath as I worked the windows halfway open. The moldy curtains waved listlessly in the breeze as the frigid air worked its way inside. The window in the laundry room was stuck pretty tight, but I did manage to open it a crack, and I hoped it was enough. With this many windows open in the back of the house, it would probably drop the temperature close to actual freezing. It almost never got cold enough to snow around here, but I'd heard on the radio that there was a frost warning this week, just in time for New Year's Eve. The timing couldn't be better.

The answer had been staring me in the face this whole time. The cold. As long as I could get it cold enough, Mom would . . . keep . . . until I had time to make things look better. I didn't know that much about dead bodies, but I'd watched enough cop shows to know the cold would buy me a couple of days before things got too bad. And a couple of days might be all it took to make the difference between normal and news-worthy.

I could never keep track of the days during vacation, and it took a minute to figure out today was Tuesday. That meant I had until at least Thursday morning, maybe Friday, before Mom would have to be "discovered." I could spend the next couple of days cleaning the place up, and then go to Kaylie's to spend the night. When I came home in the morning, I could "find" Mom on the floor in a normal-looking house that contained a normal amount of stuff—lying dead in a normal position, not buried under a mountain of magazines in a house that looked like a landfill. If I closed all the windows before I left, it should warm up enough in here to make it look like she'd just died.

Two more years until I could have a normal life had seemed like an eternity, and suddenly it was like the universe was handing me a chance to have all of it ahead of schedule. There was only ten tons of garbage standing in the way.

I rushed back through the pathway, out of the kitchen, and down to my room at the end of the hall to grab my wallet. I'd need garbage bags—the big, black ones made for moments like this. As far as I knew, we didn't even own any. I stood in my open doorway and felt my heartbeat slow and the knot in my stomach loosen. I kicked the door shut behind me, blocking out the smell and the mess, and took a deep breath.

The flutter of panic that had been whirling in my head was being replaced by something else. I felt a little guilty for the warmth of optimism that was spreading throughout my body at a time when I should have been devastated, but there it was. For once in my life, I was in charge. If I worked hard enough, I could keep Kaylie and Josh and the glimmer of a normal life that had started to form.

Was it selfish? Absolutely. It wasn't like I could do anything to save Mom at this point, but I could do something to help me. But I wasn't *just* doing it for me. I was doing it for Phil and his girlfriend and Sara too. In a way, I was even doing it for Mom. She could still be the hardworking single parent everybody thought she was. Now Nadine and everybody else who knew her wouldn't have to change their memories.

As I looked around my bedroom at the clean surfaces and

my neatly made bed, I could feel some energy return deep inside. I could do this. I didn't help Mom last night, but I could help all of us now.

Taking one last look around my room, I gathered strength from the peaceful space. Mom was dead—there was nothing I could do about that. Local history would remember us either as that garbage-hoarding freak family on Collier Avenue, or as the nice oncology nurse with the lovely children.

It was up to me to decide which one was our truth.

chapter 4

11:00 a.m.

Our street was one of those that had ridden the roller coaster of good times and bad, and it showed in the little details, like fine wrinkles around an otherwise pretty face. You could tell it had once been a really nice neighborhood because the houses were set back from the street and most of them had big porches, but the old Toyota up on blocks in the Harveys' driveway and the weeds that choked out any grass in the yard on the corner told a different story. The houses were old, but mostly in a good way, and each one had a big yard, which meant the neighbors weren't so close that they were always peeking in your windows. Keeping nosy neighbors away was a good thing as far as I was concerned.

I shifted the bag of cleaning supplies to my left hand and unlocked the front door with my right. As the door swung open, bits of mail caught in the bottom and made a scratching sound along the tile floor. I kicked the mail to the side, where it joined the pile from yesterday.

Standing in the hallway, I stopped to listen. I wasn't sure

what I was listening for, but the whole house was silent. Dead silent. I knew Mom was lying in the back hallway, but just for one moment, I wanted to pretend I was coming through the door for the first time today. Mom was at work, I was coming home from Kaylie's with the warmth of Josh's arm still on my shoulders, and none of this was my problem. Yet.

Our entry hall was wide, with the living room on the right and the dining room on the left. Piles of belongings, newspapers, and green plastic bins draped with clothing started at the edges of each room and marched toward the center until the only way to maneuver through the stuff was to turn sideways and pray you would reach your destination unscathed.

On the other side of the living room was the fireplace mantle, which held a brown, spindly potted plant that had been dead for years and a couple of framed pictures. I stood on my tiptoes so I could see them better. The picture on the right was my school picture from fourth grade. I was wearing my sweatshirt jacket, and Mom had gotten mad at me because I forgot to take it off for picture day so my new shirt would show. I remember when Aunt Jean put the picture in the big gold frame and set it on the mantle. It was the last time she was in our house, before Mom banished her forever.

The house wasn't nearly as crowded back then—the kitchen still worked, mostly, and both bathrooms were usable. The piles were just starting to accumulate, and most weren't any taller than my head.

Even though I was only nine when it happened, I'd been able to figure out that the car accident was bad. Mom didn't come home after work that first night, so Sara had come back to stay with us for a few days, not letting us forget she was doing us a favor. Phil was five years older than me, but Sara was almost ten years older—somewhere between a sister and something else, and she was always looking for an excuse to boss us around. She had already graduated from high school and had moved to San Francisco, so she couldn't stay with Phil and me for very long without missing work. She left after a few days, and Aunt Jean came to stay with us until Mom got better.

I was helping Aunt Jean with her suitcase when she got her first look at the inside of our house.

"Oh my God," she said. Her hand flew to her mouth as she surveyed the clutter that covered most horizontal surfaces and lined the edges of every room.

I put her suitcase down on the tile floor, thinking she'd seen a mouse or something. "What?" I looked around frantically.

Aunt Jean turned to look into the dining room. "This . . . this place," she said. "Look at all this junk. My God, there's crap everywhere." She turned to me. "How long has it been like this?"

I looked around the living room and shrugged. There were some piles of clothes that had never been folded and put away, and Mom did like to save newspapers in case she missed an important article. The sink was clogged, so the dishes hadn't been done for a while, but I really didn't see the problem.

Aunt Jean ran her fingers through her hair as she rushed from room to room, looking at the piles of clothes on every bed, and the mildew that was starting to become a permanent fixture in the bathrooms. I finally caught up with her in Mom's room as she sat in the one tiny clear spot on the bed with her head in her hands.

"Auntie Jean?" I said quietly.

She looked up at me, tears running down her face, and shook her head. "I had no idea . . . I should have known because of Mama that Joanna could get this bad. But I really had no idea."

I stood there quietly waiting for her to say something else. Mom cried a lot like this after Dad left us, but other than that, I hadn't seen many grown-ups freaking out before. Aunt Jean reached out and pulled me to her, grabbing me around the waist and holding me tight.

"I'm so sorry," she said over and over. "I had no idea."

As I stood there, wrapped in her arms, I decided maybe I'd gotten it wrong. Maybe Mom was hurt worse than I'd thought, or maybe she was already dead. We were supposed to go and see her that afternoon, but now it was too late. I turned this thought over and over in my head until I believed it was true with all the conviction a nine-year-old can gather, and tears started spilling out of my eyes and down my face. Mom was gone. Mom was gone, and I was going to have to go live with someone else, away from my school and everything I knew. I didn't want to go and live with Dad—Mom said that Daddy was the devil and that he never really loved any of us. If he did, he'd never have abandoned us like he did. Even worse, maybe he'd only let one of us live there, and I wouldn't have anybody at all who cared about me. My tears turned from silent tracks into loud sobs that made my whole body shake.

"Oh, sweetheart," Aunt Jean said. She held me away from her so she could see my face. She rubbed my tears away with the palm of her hand and smoothed my hair back from my forehead. "It's going to be okay."

I tried to swallow the hiccups that had started in my chest

so I could speak. "Are we going to have to live somewhere else?" I finally squeaked out between sobs.

Aunt Jean looked around the room. "No. No, honey. We'll get this straightened out in no time. Your mom is going to have to stay in the hospital for a couple of weeks—that should give us just enough time to have this place spic and span."

I blinked back a fresh set of tears in disbelief. "She's coming home?" I said. "I thought she was dead."

Aunt Jean laughed and gave me another hug. "No, honey, she's not dead." She took another look around the room. "Your mom is one hell of a slob, but she's definitely not dead."

As we drove to pick up mom from the hospital on the last day, Aunt Jean turned to us. "Now remember, we want this to be a surprise, so don't say anything until we get home." She sounded cheerful and confident, but she looked nervous as she said it, her hands gripping the steering wheel so tight her knuckles were white.

I looked down at my own hands. Aunt Jean had told us to wear gloves as we cleaned and scoured every surface in the house, but I could never get any gloves that fit right, so I'd just gone without. Now my hands were an angry red, and all of my nails were broken down to the bare edges.

But it had been worth it. For two weeks, Aunt Jean and Phil and I had dragged bags of trash out to the Dumpster she had rented that stood sentry in front of the house. The plumber had been called, and every dish shone from its place in the cupboard. Once the floors and tables were clear, we had sorted through the closets and drawers. Finally, every surface was scrubbed and bleached until there wasn't a speck of mold left in the whole house. Aunt Jean had done most of the work; I could see the light from the hallway streaming under my door late into the night. It was like she couldn't sleep until the house was spotless.

Phil was chewing on his fingernail and staring out the window as the streets rushed by. "Auntie Jean," he said quietly.

I could see her glance at him in the rearview mirror. "What's on your mind, babe?"

"Do you . . . do you think she's going to like it?" he asked.

Aunt Jean glanced at the road, and then back to him. "We did it out of love," she said. "How can your mom not like something we did out of love?"

"Then why couldn't we tell her?" I said. "Or Sara?" Sara hadn't bothered to come back once Aunt Jean showed up, spending all her time either at the hospital or at her apartment.

"Well," she said. "Your sister is busy with her own life, and your mom might have felt bad because she couldn't help. You know that even though she's getting out of the hospital today, she's going to need lots and lots of rest. Isn't it better that she recuperates in a nice, clean house with all of us there to take care of her?"

"I guess," Phil said, not looking convinced. I didn't know what he was so worried about—it's not like we did anything bad. He shot a glance at me and I shrugged.

"Watch your step, Joanna," Aunt Jean said as she guided Mom's walker up to the house. "Put your wheels on the stoop and then take the step up slowly."

"I've got it," Mom said, clearly frustrated at having to rely on someone else for help.

"I just don't want you to fall," Aunt Jean said.

Mom stopped her slow progress up the walk and leaned on the handles, her breathing coming hard, like she'd just run a marathon. "I know. I'm sorry. I really appreciate everything you've done for the kids the past few weeks. You must be anxious to get home."

Aunt Jean leaned over and kissed her sister on the cheek. "It was nothing. I know you'd do the same for me. The only thing that matters now is that you get better."

Phil and I walked behind the two of them, me carrying several bunches of flowers from her hospital room and Phil carrying Mom's small suitcase.

I was so excited I felt like I was going to explode. We'd worked so hard to get everything finished—even the big Dumpster had been taken away just this morning, leaving only two parallel scrapes in the street to show it had ever been there. "Can we tell her now?" I asked. I was practically jumping up and down, and wished they would hurry up and get to the door.

"Tell me what?" Mom smiled. It was probably the first smile I'd seen since her accident. The worry lines in her forehead had gotten so deep they looked like scars from a lifetime of hurt.

Aunt Jean concentrated on finding the right key on her key ring. "Oh, just a little surprise we cooked up for you."

Phil hung back and didn't say anything.

"Open the door already!" I practically shouted.

Mom had a confused smile on her face as Aunt Jean swung the door open.

I scooted past the two of them and into the sparkling hallway that still smelled faintly of pine cleaner. "Ta da!"

Mom placed the front legs of the walker in the hallway and pulled herself into the house. She took two tentative steps and stopped, craning her neck to see into the dining room and then back to the living room. "Oh no," she said quietly. The walker rattled on the tiles as she tried to hurry down the hallway. Her voice got louder and more frantic as she went. "Oh no . . . oh no . . . oh no!"

Aunt Jean followed behind her, but Mom didn't seem to notice. "Now, Joanna, it just needed a bit of sprucing up in here," she said. "It's no big deal, really. Joanna?"

Mom continued her noisy scraping along the hallway until she got to her bedroom. One hand gripped the walker as the other flew to her mouth. "Where are they? Where are all my things?" She turned and started back down the hallway to where Aunt Jean had stopped. "My papers and photos? All of my quilting supplies—some of those fabrics are irreplaceable!"

"You need to calm down," Aunt Jean said. "We kept everything that was valuable. It's all put away. The kids did such a wonderful job—"

"The kids? You made the kids do this to me?" Mom looked at Phil and me. He hadn't even made it through the doorway yet—he stood outside with his eyes planted firmly on the ground.

"Phil and Lucy worked so hard trying to make this place livable," Aunt Jean said, an edge creeping into her voice.

"I knew Sara would never betray me like this!" Mom said. She looked frantically around the living room. We had found the photos and put them on the mantle along with a big vase for her flowers. Mom walked up to it, and, with one swipe of her arm, pulled everything onto the floor with a crash.

Aunt Jean rushed over to the pile. "Lucy, honey, would you grab the dustpan?" she said, the waver in her voice the only sign she wasn't as calm as she looked. She took my fourth-grade picture and gently placed it back on the mantle.

Mom turned on me. "You'll do no such thing," she said. She turned back to Aunt Jean, gripping the handles of her walker so tight her arms were shaking. "Where is everything? I want everything back in this house by tonight," she said.

Aunt Jean straightened up to face her. "It's gone, Jo," she said quietly. "It's gone. You can't get it back. It was garbage. Don't you remember what it was like with Mama when we were kids? Can't you see you were living just like her?"

"I am nothing like her," Mom said, every word sounding like it had come from the center of her body. She was practically spitting with anger. "I am a *collector*. Everything in this house has . . . had a purpose and a meaning. How dare you come in here and get rid of my treasures!"

I hugged the wall as I crept back onto the porch where Phil was still standing.

Aunt Jean's eyes were wet as she tried to reason with Mom. "But all of the mold and mildew—and what I found in the refrigerator! It's not healthy living like this. Don't you remember when we were kids? What if their friends found out?" She swung around and pointed at me. "Do you want them to make fun of her too? I remember what it was like even if you don't."

"Get out!" Mom started screaming at her. "Get out! I will not tolerate this in my own house. You took advantage of me! You probably stole my things for yourself. Get out!"

Aunt Jean still didn't move. "Joanna, calm down. It's going to be okay. Look around at your beautiful house."

"Get out!" Mom screamed at Aunt Jean one last time and, with all the effort she could muster, swung the walker at her. One leg caught Aunt Jean under the eye as she scrambled out of the way.

"Fine!" Aunt Jean said as she made her way to the door, her fingers pressed to her rapidly swelling face. "You're on your own from now on. You don't want help, you just live here and drown in your own filth." As she passed me in the doorway, she placed a hand on my cheek. "Take care of each other," she said. "I'll do everything I can to help." And then she was gone.

Mom lay crumpled in a heap on the living room floor, tears streaming down her cheeks. I walked over to try to help her up, but she swatted my arm away.

"I don't need you," she said. She looked at Phil still standing in the doorway. "Either of you."

We both watched silently as she dragged herself to the coffee table and used that to swing herself onto the chair. That night, she spent the first of many nights sleeping on our old green recliner.

These past few years, her room had gotten so cluttered and her bed hidden under such a huge mountain of clothes, it was almost impossible to sleep there. Her life in this house had shrunk down to the space around that old recliner.

Over time, Mom got less angry at Phil and me, but things were never the same as before. Sara loved to suck up to Mom and tell her over and over how she would have never let us do it if she had known. If any of us ever wondered who the favorite was, we didn't anymore.

Aunt Jean might have tried to help, but I only talked to her a couple of times after that. She would call when she knew

Mom was at work and ask me how things were. I'd tell her they were okay, and she'd tell me she was sorry, but I always tried to get off the phone quickly. I felt so bad about betraying Mom that I didn't dare keep in touch after she told us not to. Little by little, Mom eliminated almost every "outsider" from our lives. It was better this way, she used to tell us. The only people you can trust were right here in the immediate family. Phil just spent as much time as possible away from home until he could leave for good. That's what we all did—waited until we could leave for good.

It took three people and two solid weeks to clean out Mom's mess. It took her less than six months to return it to squalor.

chapter 5

11:10 a.m.

Two weeks. As much as I tried to be positive, I couldn't ignore the fact it had taken us two entire weeks to clean out the house back then, and there were three of us doing it—now there was just me and a whole lot more stuff.

Mom was lying in the back of the house, but at least she was in the hallway. This way, I only had to clear the places the paramedics would see as they dragged the stretcher through the house to get her. Any room that had a door could be shut away from prying eyes, and I could deal with them later. I didn't have to do the whole house in the next couple of days. Just the visible parts.

Still, I had no idea where to start, and taking it in as a whole made it look impossible. But impossible wasn't an option.

Mom always said you eat an elephant a bite at a time, so I tried to concentrate on one little part of one room. I walked back to the front door and turned around, trying to find the spots that would make the most difference. I tried to see it as someone new would, someone who hadn't gotten used to seeing piles and piles of junk as they expanded over the years until they were as much a part of the house as the couch or dining room table. Not that you could actually see the couch or the table under all the garbage.

Obviously, I would have to start with the front hallway. At some point, Mom had covered this part of the mound with a sheet so it wouldn't look so bad in case someone caught a glimpse of what was inside the house. Cautiously, I lifted a corner of the sheet and peeked underneath. As far as I could tell, it was the same assortment of clothes, mail, newspapers, and plastic grocery bags resting on the ever-popular green bins that were scattered through the house.

As I put the sheet back down, I noticed a familiar box about halfway down the pile. I pulled it out and lifted the cover to see that the slippers were still in there, just as new as they had been when I'd given them to her for her birthday a couple of years ago. I'd looked hard to find some that matched her old ratty ones almost exactly, and she'd seemed happy when she opened them. But here they were in a mound of junk, while her old nasty ones were still snug on her feet.

I walked back into the dining room and opened the first box of trash bags. The bag made a sharp snapping sound as I shook it open—it was the sound of efficiency and organization and somehow it made me feel a little better.

The top of the nearest pile held the mail from the past few weeks. The whole place was like some sort of archaeology site—the layers closest to the top had the most recent stuff, while the layers on the bottom were probably six or seven years old. As I crammed the fliers and ads into the first bag, I started to feel guilty about just throwing it all away. Mom always said she'd recycle all this stuff—it's one of the reasons she had for keeping it. I could at least recycle the newspapers, but they would be too heavy for the garbage bags. Luckily, we had a huge stack of boxes in the garage. Mom never threw away a good box.

On my way to the garage, I tried not to look toward her room, but I couldn't help it. Something moved and I jumped, but it was only a fly. A big, shiny, greenish black fly. It sat on a yellow magazine, changing and shifting direction every few seconds like it was waiting for something to happen. Weren't flies supposed to be hibernating or something when it was this cold out?

I couldn't stand to see it there, rubbing its legs together in anticipation, so I made my way back to the front hallway and grabbed the sheet that was covering the monster pile by the door. With the grimy sheet over my shoulder, I inched my way back down the hall until I was standing at Mom's feet. In one quick movement I flung the sheet over her like it was some sort of magic trick. And it worked. Mom had used the sheet to make the junk in the hallway disappear, and now I used it to make her disappear. The fly was out of luck.

It felt much better to have Mom all covered up, so I worked my way to the garage. It took several minutes of digging to get a couple of boxes from the pile that was stacked against the garage wall. The garage was what the house aspired to. It was so packed full of stuff that it seemed like there was no way to cram even one more tiny item into the overwhelmed space. There wasn't even a real path through the stuff anymore. If something needed to be stored in the garage, most of the time we just stood in the doorway and tossed it as far into the mess as we could. A long time ago, someone had put plywood up in the rafters in an attempt at organization, but now everything that was up there just made the beams in the ceiling sag until they almost met the piles on the ground. The whole space had an air of impending doom.

As I turned to walk back up the concrete steps and into the house, I caught a glimpse of a silver fender sticking out of the pile. My car. At least Mom said it would be once she got it out of here and fixed it up. It was really Mom's old car that she'd put in here when she'd bought the new one a couple of years ago. Maybe someday I could dig the car out and get it running, or even use hers. I could finally get my license and feel like I was free. It would sure beat having to ask Kaylie's mom for a ride everywhere.

I grabbed the boxes from the garage and dragged them back down the pathway to the front door. It only took ten minutes to go through one big stack, recycling most of it and throwing the rest in one of the garbage bags. I picked up the box to take this first load outside, but when I got to the hallway, the sides were blocked by the stacks of newspapers and magazines—the path was way too narrow for me to carry the box through the kitchen and out the back door. I could feel my muscles straining as I stood in the front hallway trying to decide what to do with the heavy, awkward box. The last thing I needed was to draw attention to myself by carrying the bags and boxes through the front door, but until I'd made the main path wider, it was going to be impossible to carry them out through the back.

I checked my watch. Eleven thirty on a Tuesday morning. The only people who would really be around were old Mrs. Raj next door and maybe TJ from across the street, unless his mom put him in some sort of day camp during vacation. I decided going out the front was worth the risk—mainly because I had no other choice.

As I set the box down behind the garage, I felt like I had begun to accomplish something. I was even sweating from the exertion, despite the cold weather, so I took off my jacket and hung it on the back of the front doorknob as I came back in.

I was feeling even more accomplished as I hauled the next box out the front door. I heard the skateboard wheels scraping the concrete before I saw him.

"Hey," TJ said as he kicked the back of his skateboard so it landed in his hand. "Whatcha doin'?"

I shifted the weight of the box to my hip and turned to him. "Just some cleaning."

"My mom always does that after Christmas so she can make room for the new stuff," he said.

"Well, there you go." I turned to walk away.

"Can I help?" he asked.

I sighed and stopped walking. I really liked him, but the last thing I needed was a kid hanging around asking questions. "No, TJ. Not really. I'm doing fine on my own."

"Are you getting rid of anything good?"

"I don't know," I said. "How about I let you know when I'm finished."

"I can go through it with you," he said. "Come on, I'm totally bored."

I looked up and down the empty street. "Aren't there any other little kids around today?"

TJ tipped his helmet back on his head with one hand. "I'm not a little kid," he said. "I'm in third grade."

"Listen," I said. "Anyone I babysit on a regular basis is a little kid. Go find someone else to bother. I'm really busy here."

"Fine." TJ's shoulders slumped as he turned to walk down my driveway. Great. Now his feelings were hurt. I really did not have time for this.

"Hey, T," I called after him. "How about I make a pile for you to go through later? If I find any cool stuff Phil left behind I'll give you first pick."

He shrugged without turning around, but dropped his skateboard on the sidewalk and, with a running start, rolled around the corner and out of sight. I took that as a yes.

Back inside, I felt good, like I was making progress. As I stuffed the boxes full of paper, I grabbed a bag labeled "Scrub City"—Mom's favorite clothing store. Sure enough, it was filled with colorful nursing scrubs with the tags still on, and I wondered how long ago she'd bought these. I pulled out a shirt that was covered with *Simpsons* characters all dressed for Christmas—Homer had on a Santa hat and Lisa's saxophone was covered in lights. Mom always found the most obnoxious scrubs to wear because she said it made her people feel better to look at something cheerful. She never called them her patients, always her "people." I guess calling them patients would make it more obvious that a lot of them were never going home again. Maybe after, I could take these down to her work and let the other nurses have them. Sort of like Mom's legacy.

I'd gone down to the hospital with her for one of those "Take Your Daughter to Work" days a couple of years ago. I'd been there lots of times, usually parked at the nurses' station with a supply of pens and pads of paper with the names of pharmaceutical companies written on the top, but we never stayed more than a couple of minutes—just long enough for her to pick up her paycheck or see to one of her people quickly. I'd spent half a day there once when the daycare lady didn't show up, but I'd never seen her actually work before.

I'd expected the same cranky, irritated person I saw at home every day, but once she stepped through the sliding doors, she was different. Her face softened, and there was a slight smile on her lips as we approached the floor where she worked.

"Good morning, Mr. Evans," she said to a tall, skinny bald man as we got off the elevator. He was wearing red plaid pajamas with a matching red plaid robe and gripped a tall pole that held an assortment of IV bags. Tubes snaked from under his robe and attached to the bags as he wheeled the contraption along beside him.

"Good morning, Joanna," he said, his gaunt face assembling into a slight smile. He turned to me. "Do we have a new nurse on the ward?" I'd picked the least objectionable pair of scrubs in her closet, but I was still mortified to be seen with roller-skating penguins all over my shirt. Mom said if I was going to miss an entire day of school, I had to look the part.

"This is my daughter Lucy," she said, putting her arm around me like it was the most natural thing in the world. "She's come to see what we do here all day, so you boys better behave yourselves." She winked at him as she said it. Arm around my shoulder? Winking? It was like Mom had been taken over by some kindly nurse alien.

"Aw, come on, Jo," he said, winking back. "That's no fun now, is it?"

"Just see what you can do for the next few hours, okay?" Mom patted his arm as he continued his slow shuffle down the hallway.

Mom turned to me. "Let's get you settled, shall we?" she said brightly, like we were going to spend the day at Disneyland instead of in a hospital cancer ward. We went to the nurses' station and put our purses in the locked filing cabinet that held her stuff. She introduced me to the other nurses on the floor, reminding me which ones I'd met over the years. She kept saying, "My youngest, Lucy," as if she was actually proud of that fact rather than thinking I was a liability.

For the next few hours, I followed her around the floor, watching her check charts and stick needles into IV tubes. Mom chatted with the people in the beds like they were old friends— asking about their kids or their husbands, talking about the latest episode of some cop show they both watched, even while she had to pump some chemical into their bodies that was bound to make them feel even worse than they did already. She let me carry the bottles of medicine and once let me hold an IV bag, but most of the time I felt embarrassed for being upright and healthy while all these people were so sick.

Late in the afternoon, we stopped by a half-closed door to a darkened room. Mom pushed it open, but turned to me. "I'm going to take this one alone, okay? Do you mind waiting here for just a minute? I'll be right back."

"Yeah. Okay," I said. She sounded so calm and reasonable I almost didn't know how to react. It was like we'd spent the day reading a script of how a good mother-daughter team should communicate. I couldn't help watching through the crack in the door as she talked softly to someone I couldn't see behind a curtain. Instead of the harsh florescent lights and blaring TV in the rest of the rooms, this one was lit by a small bedside lamp and had soft classical music playing in the background. I could see Mom standing at the foot of the bed and stroking the tops of the person's feet under the blankets.

"Your mama is good at what she does," her boss, Nadine, said, coming up behind me so softly I jumped.

"Oh, I was just, uh . . . she asked me to wait out here," I said, looking as guilty as I felt for peeking.

"It's fine, sugar," she said. "Mrs. Collingwood is one of your mama's special people. No family or even many friends around, so Joanna tends to spend a little extra time. Mrs. Collingwood's been in and out of here so much over the years that we told her last time we'd issue her a FastPass so she could go right to the head of the line." She looked at my blank face. "That was a joke."

I smiled weakly, but it seemed wrong to joke in a place that held this much pain. "I got it," I said.

Nadine reached out to pat my shoulder. "Been a hard day for you?"

I shrugged. It had been weird to see Mom so efficient, so capable of taking care of other people when I knew deep down she was a failure at taking care of her kids. Maybe she used up all the good stuff before she got home. The person Nadine saw at work every day and the person who slept in her robe on our green recliner every night seemed like two different people.

Nadine peeked through the crack in the door. "I'd tell you it gets easier, but it doesn't, really." She nodded toward Mom.

"Joanna is one of the most caring and knowledgeable nurses I've ever worked with. Plenty of times she's caught things even the doctors have missed." She turned to me. "Think you'll ever become a nurse? Or a doctor?"

"Oh, I don't know," I said, but that was really just to be polite, because I did know. Nursing was one more way I wouldn't be like Mom when I got older.

I could hear Mom's shoes squeak as she turned to leave the room, so I took a couple of steps away from the door. She forced a smile as she closed the door behind her.

"She's having a tough time," Mom said to Nadine. She looked at a chart in her hands. "I tell you what, Lucy," she said. "School would be almost over by now, so what's say I run you home on my break and then come back here for a while?"

"Okay," I said.

"You come back and see us anytime," Nadine said, and gave me a quick hug.

"Thanks, I will."

Mom drove me home, and then stayed at the hospital until way after I went to bed. As I lay there alone in the dark that night, I wondered if you had to be sick or dying to get Mom's full attention. I never asked, but I always pictured Mrs. Collingwood dying that night, with Mom sitting next to her, talking softly and rubbing her feet as she slipped away. It was an image I tried to keep with me whenever she was being particularly unreasonable or screaming her head off at how stupid I was. I would remember back to the day I was proud of her, and somehow that made it not so bad.

chapter 6

12:30 p.m.

Once the first boxes were filled and put away, I had to drag more empty ones out of the garage. I tried to look at it as though I was getting rid of two things at once, and from the looks of the garage, Mom probably had enough cardboard boxes to handle most of what was in the house. She always said she could start sorting through her things once she got enough boxes. I was guessing she finally had enough.

My stomach started rumbling as I picked my way through the piles in the front hallway, and I wished I'd gotten something to eat when I'd gone out before. As I was lifting a pile of newspapers from the far corner of the living room, I stumbled and the stack hit something that made a faint tinkling sound. I tossed some newspapers off the top and saw the familiar dark wood. Our old piano. It had been so long since I'd seen it, I'd actually forgotten we had one. Shoving years of junk off the keyboard, I hit a few notes that were wildly out of tune but left me with a strangely satisfied feeling inside.

Somewhere in a distant corner of my mind, I remembered

being a really little kid and sitting with my back against the side of the piano, feeling the notes run up my spine as Mom's hands flew over the keyboard. When Daddy first left us, Mom spent all her free time playing the piano. She didn't play lullabies or pretty music, though. Her songs were loud and harsh and demanded that you pay attention. I would sit for what seemed like hours with my head just barely touching the dark wooden piano leg, watching as her feet worked the pedals furiously. I used to think that someday she would pedal that piano so hard it would start up, crash through the wall, and drive off down the street.

My fingers left prints in the dust that had settled on the faded wood. Nobody had touched the piano in years. After Mom stopped crying all the time, she didn't seem to need the music anymore. I wondered if she buried the piano to forget about it, or if once it was buried, she never thought about music at all.

Over the next hour, I filled six more boxes of various sizes and deposited them behind the garage. That space was starting to look fuller, but I wasn't seeing much difference inside the house. Plus, my arms were aching from all that lifting. I shook them out to try to get the blood flowing again.

As I looked around, I started to notice the clothes. There were clothes everywhere—some on hangers dangling off furniture and doorknobs, some in plastic bags with the tags still on them, and some draped here and there over stacks of other things, like someone had discarded a shirt or pants and was coming back to get them in a minute.

I picked up one of the black trash bags and started grabbing at the clothes that were within reach. Mom went shopping almost every day looking for deals, but we didn't go out together very often. She always said I slowed her down because I stopped to look at everything, and she had a very cutthroat method of getting through a store. It was almost as if she wasn't interested in what she bought: the real point of the trip was the discount she got. She thought thrift stores were invented just for her.

There was a large red Macy's bag underneath a pile of shirts in the living room. I stuffed the shirts into the giveaway bag and reached for the Macy's bag that was full of something, but it didn't feel like clothes. Pulling the handles apart, I spotted six or seven wallets, all the same style but in different colors. I recognized them immediately because I had a green one exactly like them in my purse.

We'd been on one of our rare mother-daughter shopping trips when I'd found the wallets on the sale rack last year. They came in a dozen colors ranging from hot pink (definitely not me) to more muted sage and cobalt blue. They were perfect because they weren't filled with spaces for photos of the friends I didn't have. Just room for money and a license if I ever got one. I was looking at the display when Mom came up behind me.

"Ooh, these are nice," she said. She picked up a pink one and opened it to see the inside.

"Yeah, I need a new wallet," I said warily. I never knew if Mom would be in a bad mood and accuse me of wasting money even if it was mine. "I've been using my black one for such a long time, it's falling apart. What do you think, green or blue?"

Mom took both of them from me and looked from one to the other. "They're both so pretty." She looked at me out of the corner of her eye. "You know, Christmas is just around the corner. Maybe Santa can bring you a new wallet, and you can save your money."

"You don't have to do that," I said. "Besides, these are expensive." I'd learned not to expect too much for Christmas or my birthday. Mom always seemed to have some sort of financial crisis right before a major holiday.

"They're not that much," Mom said. She turned the blue one over and looked at the back. "They're already forty percent off—and I'll bet they'll go down more closer to the holidays. What color do you think Santa should bring?"

I smiled at her. Sometimes, mom could be cool like in the old days. "I don't know. Why doesn't he just surprise me?" I put both wallets down on the display. "But Santa shouldn't bring me pink."

"I'll let him know," she said.

On Christmas morning, we went over to Aunt Bernie and Uncle Jack's house to open presents. They weren't really related to us, but they'd been friends with Mom since before she and Dad got divorced and were the closest thing we had to family nearby. They didn't have any kids, and we'd been opening our presents at their house since I was little. Best of all, they had a huge house in the hills, so there was always room to play with whatever new toy we'd been given.

I still had a few presents left to open when Mom handed me a big, square box. Things shifted inside when I shook it, and I couldn't imagine what was in there. As I tore off the wrapping, Mom sat excitedly on the sofa waiting for me to see what was inside. I lifted the lid to find not just a green wallet, not just a blue wallet, but a bunch of wallets in all different colors scattered in the box.

"Do you like them?" Mom asked, clapping her hands like a little kid. "Remember, we saw the wallets in Macy's that day?"

I set each one out on the carpet in front of the fireplace. There were eight of them, in every color except pink. I looked at Mom. "I remember," I said. "But I thought you were only going to get one."

"Well, they were such a good deal, I decided to get a few," she said, waving the cost away with her hand. "You know I can never pass up a bargain. Your present is that you get to choose whichever one you want."

I picked up the green one. "Thanks, Mom. But what are you going to do with the rest of these?" I could see Aunt Bernie staring at us with a strange look on her face.

"I don't know," she said. "People always need gifts, or I'll take the rest back." She leaned over and kissed me on the cheek. "I just want you to be happy."

Aunt Bernie laughed. "Well, Joanna, my birthday is in February. Just remember I've got my eye on the gold one over there."

"You got it," Mom said, laughing like it was all a big joke.

As I sat there with the Macy's bag in my hand, I realized she'd never intended to return any of these. She always bought things for people and then could never remember where she'd put them, so they just got swallowed up with everything else—the gold wallet meant for Aunt Bernie was sitting right on top. Bernie and Jack always left for a long vacation in Hawaii after

Christmas, but maybe I'd surprise her with it when they got back.

I turned it over to look at the price tag. Fifty dollars. Even if she'd gotten these at half price, it still meant there was almost two hundred dollars' worth of wallets in just this one bag.

I sat down on the recliner and picked at the pile on the couch. Who knew what was in the rest of the house? How many more Macy's bags was I going to find? How many shirts still had their tags? How many pairs of shoes did she buy and then toss in a pile, never to think of them again? I could feel myself starting to get angry, but I tried to get back to work. I didn't have time to feel things right now. I tossed the Macy's bag to the side and figured I'd decide what to do with it later. There was one last box full of paper sitting in the hallway, so to make room I grabbed it and yanked open the front door.

"Hello?" The delivery driver stood on the porch with an equally big box in his arms, his eyes peering over the top of it.

Startled, I dropped my own box in the doorway, and then shoved it out of the way so I could shut the front door quickly. My heart was pounding, but I tried to look calm.

"I'm sorry I scared you," he said. He shifted the weight of the box to one hip and glanced down at his clipboard. "I'm looking for Mrs. Tompkins."

From the lack of alarm on his face, I didn't think he'd seen anything inside. At least he wasn't giving anything away. I looked back at the door to make sure it was shut. "You, um, you just missed her."

He nodded at the door. "Do you live here?"

"Yes," I said.

He held the clipboard out to me. "Would you mind signing on that line at the bottom?"

I scribbled something that looked like my name at the bottom of his list. He took a step toward the front door. "This is really heavy—how about I bring it in for you? I can just drop it inside the door."

"No!" I said too quickly and then caught myself. "No, it's fine. I'm just going to put this box in the recycling. I'll get it when I come back." I pointed to a spot along the wall. "You can just set it there for now."

"Are you sure? I'd be happy to bring it—"

"I'm sure. It's fine." I picked up my box and watched as he set his down by the door. "Thanks."

"No problem. You have a good day."

I waited until he got back into his big brown truck and drove away. After dumping my box out back, I examined the delivery on the porch and wondered what on earth Mom could have ordered this time. It was huge and had the logo of that TV shopping network on the side, like most of the empty boxes I was pulling out of the garage.

The street was quiet, so I took the keys out of my pocket and sliced open the tape that held the top shut. As I peeled back the flaps, I could see what it was Mom had to order just three days after Christmas. I pulled it partway out of the carton until I could see what it looked like, then let it slip right back inside.

A mixer. One of those huge red mixers that sat on a counter, with a big silver bowl, and whipped up endless batches of cookies for waiting children. For other people's waiting children, because we hadn't baked anything in this house for years. It was something for a house we didn't have, probably bought with money she always said we didn't have. But I bet she got a really good deal on it.

I kicked the box but it just wobbled a few inches. I hadn't realized how heavy it was, but the pain in my big toe felt almost satisfying. My eyes watered as I walked back into the house and slammed the door with my heel. The walls rattled, and this time I didn't feel guilty about it. With any luck, someone would come up on the porch and steal the stupid thing.

chapter 7

2:00 p.m.

I stood in the hallway, sweat beading at my hairline, my hands already aching from carrying the bags and boxes to the back. I'd been busting my butt for over three hours now, and the place didn't look any different. My eyes fell on the stacks of newspapers that still reached to the ceiling and the mountains of clothes and bags I hadn't even had time to touch. The kitchen still reeked of garbage and rot, and the paths were no wider than when I'd started. Three hours hadn't helped at all. How much would I be able to do in two days?

It's not going to work. That thought began to play over and over again in my head, pounding in my ears like I'd just run a mile. My stomach started to churn as I let the wave wash over me. I thought about giving up. It would be so easy to walk outside and dial three little numbers and end all this craziness. That would be the easy way out now, but what about later? What about tomorrow, when I had to look at Kaylie and her parents and see the disgust on their faces? When I had to see pity replace anything positive in Josh's eyes? Phil had just

moved out and gotten a normal life a couple of years ago—
could I really take it away from him?

I took a deep breath and forced myself to think about the
house the way it could be. *After.* I could replace the peeling,
gray paint with a fresh coat that would make it look almost new.
We could fix it up real nice, replacing the lingering stink with
fresh flowers on the table every week.

I could feel my heart stop racing and my breathing slow.
Thinking about the life I was going to have after was better than
Valium for calming me down. Giving up wasn't an option.
Repeating that to myself was the only way I was going to get
through this. Giving up was not an option.

Opening my eyes, I realized I'd been going about this completely the wrong way. Nobody cleaned a mess this big by picking up one little piece at a time and separating it into this pile or
that bag. Aunt Jean hadn't worried about recycling. She'd even
resorted to a shovel at one point as we filled up the Dumpster. I
had to stop seeing each little thing individually and start seeing it
as one giant thing that stood between me and the rest of my life.

Aunt Jean was right—a shovel was the only tool for this job.
Thanks to Mom's "collecting," we happened to have several
out by the shed in the back. I dragged the green trash can into
the house and set it up with a bag in a small, clear spot on the
living room floor.

Even though I knew Mom was gone, it was hard to really
believe she wasn't going to burst through the front door and
start screaming at me for touching her stuff. She wasn't going
to tell me that I never helped her and that she worked too hard
to have time for stupid things like cleaning the house. I
jammed the stuff as far down into the plastic bags as I could,

poking and punching at the clothes, papers, and scraps of fabric she valued more than she valued any of us.

Before I realized it, I had four bags full of junk that needed to go outside. Four was about the upper limit for the number of bags I could stack around the recliner before they took up all available space. When I checked out the peephole in the front door, there was an old couple slowly shuffling down the street. I tried to think about how many trips I'd taken to the backyard today. It had to be at least eight or nine. In an hour or two, people were going to start coming home from work, and the street was going to get a lot busier.

I stepped away from the door and tried to figure out another way to get this done. The hallway was still too cluttered to drag bags or boxes through, but if I continued to cart things out the front door and around the side of the house, people might get suspicious. It was getting colder in the living room, so I grabbed my jacket off the door and put it back on while I thought. Leaving the windows open in the back of the house was going to be good for keeping Mom . . . cold, but I was going to freeze in here tonight.

The windows. That was it. I grabbed one of the bags and dragged it through the living room and into the dining room. The window in that room was blocked by a small pile of boxes and bags that reached just past the windowsill. I didn't bother clearing any of it away, but just stood on top of the pile and undid the latch. Like the rest of the house, the windows were old, and this one probably hadn't been opened in years. Part of it was held shut with paint, but I banged on the top of the frame until it began to inch up little by little.

When I finally had the window opened wide enough, I

stuck my head out to see what was down below. There were a few old plastic milk crates stacked against the house, but other than that it was clear. I balanced the full garbage bag on the ledge and, with a shove, sent it flying out the window where it bounced off a crate and settled onto the ground. This was the perfect solution. Not only would it save me from having to haul all this stuff out the front door for the world to see, but I could keep everything right here on the side of the house until they took Mom away.

Now it was like my body was on autopilot. All my energy was concentrated into grabbing whatever was on top of the closest stack and shoving it as far down into the trash bag as it would go. Grab a handful, shove it in the bag. Grab another handful, shove it in the bag. Bag after bag, pile after pile. I felt like I was finally making progress.

Halfway down one pile, I found what at first looked to be a large box covered with a hot pink towel. When I hit it with the back of my hand, it sounded like metal clanging together, and I realized it wasn't a box. I could see ridges under the towel that made it lie in waves along the top. Even before I pulled the towel off, the faint smell of cedar chips told me what it was and made me a little sad all over again.

I hadn't seen the hamster cage since ninth grade.

"Make sure you feed him this week," I said to Mom as I set Petey's cage down in a cleared spot on the kitchen counter. "He likes sunflower seeds and these green pellets. Also, little bits of apple and peanuts at night." Petey was curled up in a ball on his mound of cedar shavings. Every morning, he'd spend hours getting the mound just right so he could turn around three times and snuggle into it with just one ear showing.

"He eats better than I do," Mom said, peering over the top of the cage. She poked a finger in through the bars and wiggled it around. "Here, Petey Petey."

"He doesn't like it when you do that," I said to her. I was already annoyed. She never made anything easy.

"How do you know what he likes?" she asked. She waggled her finger at him one more time. "Since when did you start speaking hamster?"

"It scares him," I said. "Look, he's curling up tighter and digging in the shavings. That means he's scared."

"Maybe you don't handle him enough," she said. "Otherwise he wouldn't be such a scaredy-hamster." She pulled her finger out of the cage and stood up straight to look at me.

"Don't pick him up while I'm gone, okay? It's only two weeks—he'll be fine. Just feed him twice a day and make sure he has enough water in the bottle. I'll clean the cage when I get back." I wished I could take him with me to camp, but it would be hard to explain to the other junior counselors why I couldn't leave him at home. All Mom had to do was shove some food in his cage, and with it sitting in the middle of the kitchen, there was no way she could forget. I just kept telling myself he'd be fine.

"Don't worry about your precious rodent," she said. "I'll feed him every day. He'll be fat and happy when you get home, you'll see."

It didn't work out *exactly* that way.

"Where's Petey?" I said as I dropped my suitcase on the kitchen floor, a pile of junk mail filling the space on the counter where the cage had been.

"Oh," Mom said, looking down at the newspaper she was holding. "I was going to call you, but I didn't want to ruin your trip. He got out the other day when I was feeding him. I looked everywhere, but I couldn't find him."

"What do you mean he got out?" My eyes searched what I could see of the floor. A tiny hamster could be hiding anywhere in this house. "All you had to do was feed him. You said he'd be okay."

She put her arm around my shoulders and gave a quick squeeze. "I'm really sorry," she said. She was looking everywhere except right at me. "I only left the door open for a second so I could cut some more apple, and when I looked back he was gone."

"He really ran away?"

She nodded. "I'm sure he's around here somewhere. Probably found a nice, soft corner to curl up in."

"But he was counting on me . . ." Petey was the first thing I'd ever been in charge of, and I'd let him down. He must have missed being held and stroked on the very top of his head. He must have thought I was never coming back, and he made his escape when he saw an opportunity. A sick, heavy feeling settled in my stomach and made the back of my eyelids prickle.

I got down on all fours and looked under the table and along the wall. "Here, Petey Petey." I made little kissy noises as I was calling him. "Here, Petey. I'm back. Here, Petey." Mom got down on the floor too and together we searched everywhere we could, spending the next hour at hamster level trying to find him. But we never did.

Sometimes I would see hamster droppings on the counter

or the table, and I took it as his way of telling me he was still somewhere in the house, curled up safe in a little nest he'd made for himself, only coming out at night to look for food. I'd leave a pile of peanuts on the counter for him, and little by little it would vanish, so at least I knew he was eating something.

The sharp smell from the cedar shavings in his cage brought back everything I'd felt that day when I'd come back to discover him gone. Mom must have put the cage back here in case we ever got another hamster, but we never did. It didn't seem right to bring another living thing into this house when I couldn't even manage to keep Petey safe. The water bottle was still secured to the side of the cage, but it had been dry a long time.

I carried the whole thing over to the wall where the green bins were stacked. Even if Petey was long gone, the cage was still good. Maybe when all this was over, I'd get another hamster. Or clean it out and give it to TJ. He was about the right age for a pet.

As I set the cage down on the bins, I spotted something sticking out from under the cedar chips. I shook the cage so the chips settled and I could see it better, sticking my face right up to the bars to get a good look. He wasn't curled up in a ball, but lying out straight under a thin layer of cedar chips. The skin looked dry and papery but still had a few tufts of brown hair clinging to it.

Petey.

"Oh God," I said. I looked closer to make sure, but there was really no doubt. Petey hadn't escaped at all. He'd died right in this cage while I was gone, and instead of doing something normal like burying him, or even telling me the truth, Mom must have covered up the cage and left it in the dining room like it never happened. That was her solution to everything—cover it up like it never happened.

My mind raced as I backed away from the cage containing the mummified remains of my only pet. "How could she?" I whispered. She probably forgot about him completely. Didn't feed him or even give him water. Petey trusted me and I'd totally let him down.

Without even thinking about it, I opened the top of the cage and gently wrapped him in the towel. He wasn't much more than dried skin and bones by now, but the least I could do was give him a decent burial. Grabbing the shovel, I headed outside, not caring who saw me.

On the side of the house, just under my window, was a sheltered spot next to a spindly hydrangea bush. The cold ground was hard as I stabbed at it with the shovel, but after breaking through the top layer I was able to dig a small hole, pulling out chunks of hard clay soil and piling them up in the walkway. When the hole was deep enough, I leaned the shovel against the wall and knelt down as I lowered the pink towel into it. Tucking the edges of the towel around Petey, I waited for thoughts to come—something about how I was sorry I'd left him alone, and how I'd do it differently if I had it to do again. I wished for something profound to give him a dignified send-off, but my mind just felt blank and empty. Slowly, I got up and dumped dirt back on top of him, scraping the shovel on the walkway as I scooped it up over and over again until the pink towel was gone.

When I was done, I patted the dirt down with the back of the shovel and looked at the smooth ground where my first and only pet was buried. Unless you knew, you'd never guess he was here, but maybe it would make me feel a little bit better when the bush bloomed with huge pink flowers in the spring and reminded me that Petey was in a better place.

chapter 8

3:00 p.m.

I, however, was still trapped in this crappy place. As clouds gathered outside, it grew quieter inside, and every move I made seemed to echo off the ceiling. Mom had the television going twenty-four hours a day if she was home—something to keep her company she said—so I grabbed the stereo from my room and set it up on top of a pile of papers in the middle of the kitchen. Filling the house with sound helped make it feel a little less lonely and made this crazy project seem a little less futile. Music to decontaminate by.

After I suited up in my orange rubber gloves, I stood near the sink and tried to figure out where to start in what used to be a functional kitchen. That was always the problem when you were standing in an endless pile of garbage—where to start. Regular people might leave their dirty dishes in the sink for a few hours or even a day until someone got around to washing them and putting them in the dishwasher. Once the dishwasher broke down and the plumbing backed up, our dishes sat in the sink and on the counter for years. Actual years.

The fronts of the cabinets were white once, but now looked as though they were covered in fine, brown dirt, like someone had stood in the middle of the kitchen and flung bags of potting soil all over everything. Except it wasn't potting soil. It was mold that had crept along the counters and down over the cabinets until you couldn't tell what color the cabinets were supposed to be. The mold had made its way up the tiles and the walls until the bottoms of the curtains hung heavy with black. It happened so gradually that we really didn't notice. We just stayed out of that room as much as we could and tried not to look at anything too closely. After a while, it didn't seem to matter anymore.

Getting rid of this stuff was probably some kind of biohazard. I coughed just thinking about it. Mom's breathing problems had gotten a lot worse lately—inhaling mold spores for years would do that to you. It might even kill you.

It was creepy looking closely at everything like this. If you walked by it every day you didn't notice how bad it really was. Now that I was paying attention, it was hard not to see it like Josh or Kaylie would—a disgusting mess that nobody sane would live in. Thinking about Josh just made me sadder. I don't know who I was kidding last night.

Until I got this fixed, I couldn't let anybody near it. Or near me. It was amazing Kaylie still didn't know—I'd been getting careless letting her pick me up and drop me off here. What if she'd seen how we really live? What if Josh smelled the house stink on my jacket when he put his arm around me? The heaviness started to take over as I let these thoughts race through my brain. I shook my head and tried to erase the image of him backing away from me in disgust. I couldn't think any further than right now if I had any hope of making this work.

There was no getting around cleaning the kitchen because that's where most of the stink was coming from. Like every other horizontal surface in the house, the counters were piled high with everything you'd find in a normal kitchen—times twelve. If a few empty grocery bags might come in handy some-day, Mom would save hundreds, because you never knew when the world might run out. Stacks of newspapers stood here and there waiting to be read and clipped. Empty food containers were everywhere—margarine and yogurt containers, water bot-tles, and cylinders that once held potato chips. Those were some of Mom's favorite treasures. And it's not like these just came from us. Mom "saved" empty containers from work and even random trash cans. She always said with some sort of strange, misplaced pride that she didn't go digging in other people's trash cans, but if something was sitting right there on top for all the world to see, well, then, she had an obligation to see it wasn't wasted.

I'd have to clear off some counter space to really get down to it, so I started with the stove. It was piled with miscellaneous junk as high as the range hood. A few years back the refrigera-tor broke, so Mom just piled groceries on the counter next to the stove, lining up the cans of food instead of putting them away anywhere. This would probably have been okay if she had only bought things in cans, but I was pretty sure she'd stashed things like lunch meat and fruit here too with the idea that as long as it was visible, we'd eat it quickly enough. Which was good in theory, I guess.

In order to reach the stove, I had to make a new pathway

through the piles of stuff that littered the kitchen floor. I couldn't get the trash can in here, which meant my only option was to grab a trash bag and shove anything into it that I could find. Most of the stuff in here was so destroyed by mold, I didn't bother wondering what was in the bags or boxes. It was better not to think about it, particularly if something was soggy or leaking or smelled so bad my gag reflex kicked in.

I grabbed a can of green beans from the counter beside the stove. It had an expiration date that was two years earlier. And that was probably one of the newer cans in her collection. I started to load a bag with all the canned food, but realized that cans of food would make the bag really heavy really fast. I decided to leave the rest of them on the counter. Once everything else was cleaned up, a bunch of cans sitting on a counter wouldn't look as weird. Maybe the paramedics would think she'd just gotten home from grocery shopping. If they didn't look closely, they might not figure out that the shopping trip was from five years ago.

With one hand, I held the trash bag against the stove, and with the other, I swept the containers, plastic bags, cups, and old food packages off the top. A few things missed the bag and bounced onto the floor, but I could deal with that later. I found not one, not two, but three big margarine containers full of those little plastic clips that come on bread packages. It only took one trash bag to clear most of the stove and uncover the burners. Real safe to have things piled on top of something that actually makes fire all these years, but it didn't seem to have worried Mom. On a hunch, I turned the knob for the burner, thinking that like everything else in this house it wouldn't work, but to my surprise it clicked and with a small whoosh burst into a bright blue flame.

Maybe I could start cooking in here one day, if I could get the memory of the old kitchen smell out of my brain. Once Phil moved back, I'd make meals for the two of us—I'd have to start watching the Food Network to get some ideas. Maybe I could even have people over for dinner. I could learn to make complicated casseroles and fancy appetizers. Someday, after all this had been taken care of, maybe I could even have Josh over for dinner. It would be amazing having him in *my* house for dinner without worrying about Mom and the mess. I turned the burner off and threw a stack of about fifty empty cottage cheese containers in the bag. Good thing someday wasn't all that soon.

Working my way from the stove toward the sink, I cleared the counters pretty quickly. There were a few things that might have been worth keeping, but I had to just close my eyes and toss them in the garbage. Mom had three thermoses sitting next to the sink, and I could have saved them for the Salvation Army, but the thought of having some poor unsuspecting worker actually opening one of the jars and encountering some sort of festering, mummified stew was just too cruel. In the bag they went. Opened Diet Pepsi cans that were full of something that was probably liquid once but had through the wonders of science turned solid? In the bag. A shoebox full of bottle caps? In the bag. A plastic grocery bag full of some gelatinous brown goo that was probably produce at one point? Definitely in the bag.

All the hard work made me forget about the cold wind that blew through the open windows. That and the rapid progress I was making toward the sink. Under a pile of plastic bags on the counter, I found a white dish drainer complete with dishes that had been clean once upon a time. I reached in and stroked the Underdog glass that had been the only cup I would drink from when I was little. Holding it in my hand was like discovering an old friend that I'd thought was gone forever. Underdog looked great, still bright red, white, and blue; his arm raised as he took off for parts unknown. Maybe that's what I'd liked about him—he was always ready to go somewhere new.

For the first time in more than an hour, I stopped working and carefully wiped the glass with the bottom of my shirt to remove any traces of mold. I took the rest of the dishes out of the drainer and tossed them into the garbage bag. Aside from the Underdog glass, there was nothing here I was ever going to use again. I grabbed a coffee cup that had "World's Greatest Mom" printed on it in flowery pink letters. I could still see traces of lipstick around the edge and could picture it sitting on the side of the bathroom sink full of coffee as she got ready for work. Mornings were the best time for talking to her when I was a little kid. I'd sit on the fuzzy pink toilet lid and watch Mom as she did her hair with the curling iron and put her makeup on. She'd ask about my second-grade teacher, Ms. Davis, who always had lipstick on her teeth and I'd usually tell her about something rotten Phil had done. If I was lucky, she'd spray some of her perfume in the air and let me walk through it so I could smell like her for the rest of the day. If I missed her while I was at school, I'd just sniff my sleeve and the smell of her perfume would make me feel safe. I didn't remember very much about being little, but I knew, once upon a time, Mom might have deserved the World's Greatest Mom mug.

As I held the mug over the garbage bag, I remembered with a creeping sense of dread how the dishes got into the drainer. I'd done them about four years ago, before "Garbage Girl" happened. Before I'd totally given up. It was probably the last time I'd done anything constructive in this room. In this whole house. I'd learned my lesson well.

I had planned it as a surprise for Mom. She'd been working late all week, and I'd wanted to do something that would make her life a little easier, so she'd make mine easier too. And at that point in seventh grade, I needed an easier life more than just about anything else.

Carefully pushing aside all of Mom's stuff that had started to take over the space—after the Auntie Jean episode I knew better than to throw anything away or move it more than a few inches from where she had put it—I managed to make enough room to cook dinner. Okay, *cooking* dinner might be an exaggeration, but I made a meal in that kitchen for the three of us to eat. This was before the sink stopped working and developed a permanent brown crust, and before mold had started its incessant march across all surfaces. Back when you could still eat something that had come into contact with the space and not watch for signs of botulism or trichinosis.

After school that day, I'd gone down to the grocery store on the corner and picked up one of those already cooked chickens that came in the little plastic containers. If nothing else, I knew how much Mom loved those containers with the clear plastic dome on top. For her, something as simple as a chicken container held endless possibilities. After the chicken was gone, it could be a container to take food over to a sick friend, or with a slit cut in the top, become a place to put receipts. Most likely, it

would become just another piece in her ever-growing collection of useless plastic containers. It was like she used up all
her energy thinking about possibilities for reusing stuff, so she
never got around to actually doing it. As long as something could
be labeled useful, it was allowed to stay, and if you thought
about it hard enough, you could figure out a use for just about
anything.

French bread and salad completed the meal. Phil hated
salad or anything that was naturally green, but I'd tried to make
it up to him by buying ice-cream sandwiches for dessert. Just as
I was setting the bags on the counter, Phil came in from his
room and started poking around in my bags.

"Get out of there," I said, slapping his hand away. "It's for
dinner."

"Whose dinner?"

"Our dinner. Yours, mine, and Mom's."

"What's the occasion?"

"No occasion." I pulled out the bag of salad and set it on a
clear space on the counter. "I just thought it would be good for
us to eat dinner together."

Phil opened the cupboards and found a box of Cheez-Its
that had hopefully been put in there not too long ago. After
shoving a handful of crackers in his mouth, he said, "Bull."
Tiny crumbs of cracker flew out of his mouth in a dry, orange
shower as he spoke.

"What?" I asked. He always thought he was so smart.

"Bull that you don't want anything," he said. "You're totally
fishing for something from her. What is it? You want a cat? Or a
new bike?"

I made a show of concentrating on opening the salad and

digging through the bottom cupboard for a cleanish bowl to put it in. "No."

The bag crackled as he fished around the bottom for whatever crumbs were left. "Well, I'm not falling for your 'let's be a happy family' act. You wouldn't be doing this if you didn't want something from her."

I sighed and wiped a dinner plate with a wet paper towel. "It's just that I was thinking about trying to have some girls over here. For my birthday."

Phil wiped his mouth with the back of his arm. "Why would you want to do that?"

For someone in AP classes in high school, he could be such an idiot. Was it really that different for him? Did he not care that he could never have anyone over to play video games or hang around watching late-night TV? Didn't it bother him that we always had to make excuses for why nobody could come in the house, and that we always had to figure out ways to meet people outside? Maybe boys just didn't notice those things. Unfortunately, girls did.

"A couple of the girls in my class wanted to have a sleepover. You know, have one over here because we always go to someone else's house. I've been stalling them for months, but they're starting to get suspicious."

I secretly thought that Elaina from my class had a crush on Phil—God only knows why—and that's why they all wanted to come over here. We weren't even very good friends, but she was always asking if he was going out with somebody, or if he was going to be home after school. Elaina said once that she thought Phil's curls were hot, and did I ever think he would grow his hair out. I gave her such a look that it never came up again. Luckily, he was in high school, and seventh-grade girls were totally off his radar.

Phil looked around the room. Knowing him, I figured whatever was going to come out of his mouth would be obnoxious. But he just nodded. "I can see how that would be a problem."

Buoyed by his sudden understanding, I continued letting my thoughts form into words. "So I figured I'd be nice to Mom, you know, make it easy for her, and then see if she would let us clean up a little bit—it wouldn't have to be perfect—but enough so I could have a couple of girls over just this once."

"That way, they won't have anything to say behind your back," he said. He opened the fridge and stuck his head all the way in. "Did you get any soda?"

I leaned against the sink to look at him carefully. Because he was five years older than me, we didn't do much together. He ran track at school so he was in pretty good shape, if you could think that about a brother. The fact that I wrinkled my nose made me realize you couldn't actually think that about a brother. "No soda," I said. "But there are ice-cream sandwiches in the freezer. They're shoved way up in the corner."

Phil opened the freezer and grabbed the box, sending a cascade of ziplock bags full of mysterious meat products onto the floor. "Crap," he said, hopping around on one foot. "Those things are like bricks."

I helped him pick up the bags and shoved them back into the freezer. We slammed the door quickly so nothing else could attempt an escape.

"Thanks," he said. He unwrapped the top of a sandwich

and took a bite. As he put the wrapper in our one trash can that lived under the sink, he looked me in the eye.

"About the whole Mom thing," he said. He shut the door to the cabinet and looked around the room. I felt closer to him at this moment than I'd ever felt before. We never talked about what went on in the house. Not after what happened with Aunt Jean. "Yeah," he said. "Good luck with that." He shoved the last of the ice cream in his mouth and ducked out of the room.

I was sitting at the kitchen table when Mom got home. I'd managed to clear enough space for two place settings, complete with placemats and napkins. Phil had taken a plate of food to his room, but I didn't care, as it didn't look like he was going to be all that much help.

Mom set the bags she was carrying down in the doorway to the kitchen and looked at the table. "Did I miss a holiday or something? What's all this?"

I brought the plates into the kitchen where I'd set up the food. "I just thought you could use a break," I said. I was so nervous I couldn't look at her directly. One wrong word would set her off, and I needed her to be in a good mood. The only question was what that word would be. "I picked up some dinner after school. You didn't plan anything else, did you?" Since the closest we got to family dinner was all meeting up at the pot of SpaghettiOs at the same time, it was more of a rhetorical question.

"No," she said cautiously. "I didn't. This looks nice."

"Yeah, I've got some salad and chicken. There's ice cream for dessert. I borrowed a twenty-dollar bill from the kitchen jar—is that okay?"

"It's fine." Mom washed her hands with the special antibac-terial soap she got from work. She was afraid of germs and washed her hands until they were bright red. I'm sure she would have liked to declare a national holiday for the day they invented san-itizing gel for your hands. Mom was always telling us to bundle up so we wouldn't catch cold, no matter how many times I told her that clinical studies proved it didn't make any difference, and she would never, ever, even if it was the last morsel of food on earth, take a bite from someone else's fork. "That's how you get sick," she always said. Forget about living with rotting food on the counters, mold spores in the air, and no clean dishes—just make sure you didn't share food with anyone.

We filled our plates and took them to the kitchen table, eat-ing in awkward silence like we were on a first date. My stomach was in knots, and even though I'd spent a lot of time thinking about the food, I could barely eat.

Mom spoke first. "So, how was your day?"

I speared a giant piece of lettuce and tried to decide whether to cut it or just shove it in my mouth whole. "Fine. How was work?"

"It was good." She wiped her mouth with her napkin. I watched her as we ate. She was getting those lines around her mouth that made people look like they were still smiling even after the happy thoughts had faded, and her dark hair had strands of gray shimmering through it. Mom looked over at the bags she'd dropped in the hallway, and her eyes lit up with excitement. "Oh, I stopped by Thrift Town after work, and they were having a blue-tag sale on books. Everything was a quarter, so I got some great hardback books practically free."

I thought about the four bookcases we already had stuffed

full of Mom's bargain books that none of us had ever read. The overflow books had taken up residence next to the bookcases and were now the holders of other useless stuff, as if they were some kind of towering side table. "Where are you going to put them?" I asked tentatively. I kept my eyes firmly on the rapidly cooling chicken on my plate.

"Oh, I don't know, I'll find somewhere," she said. "Some of them I bought for other people. There was one called *Mexico on $5 a Day* that I'll give to Sara for her trip next summer. It's from 1989, but I'm sure most of the information is still the same."

I took a deep breath. Here was my opening, and if I didn't take it now, I might not get another one. Dinner was coming to an end, and I knew that after that, Mom would retire to her recliner to watch TV for the rest of the night, while Phil and I stayed barricaded in our rooms. "About finding places for stuff," I said slowly. I glanced up quickly to see her expression, but she was happily cutting up chicken on her plate. "I was wondering if we could maybe do some straightening up around here this weekend."

Mom chewed and nodded slightly. "We could probably do that," she said between bites. "You know I've been busy organizing the drawers in the coffee table. There was so much good stuff in there, you wouldn't believe it." Maybe she would understand, after all.

"Well, I was thinking about more than just the coffee table," I said. I could hear myself starting to talk more quickly. Once the words were out, I wouldn't be able to take them back again, so I just had to move forward. Like taking a Band-Aid off in one quick motion. "I was thinking maybe we could take some of the newspapers and magazines to the recycling center and go through some of the stuff that's starting to pile up in the living room."

Mom's chewing slowed. "I don't know about that," she said. She glanced down the hallway with a worried look. "I haven't had a chance to go through all of the newspapers yet. There might be something in there I really need, and if we just toss them all, I might miss it. And stuff is not starting to 'pile up' in the living room. I know where everything is, and it's all very necessary. I have my quilting supplies for when I start quilting again, and there are the clothes I'm sorting through for the charity drive at church."

"There is such a thing as the Internet, Mom." I could hear sarcasm creeping into my voice, but I couldn't stop it. I could feel her pushing back, and I wasn't ready to give up yet. "You can pretty much find everything you need there, you know. You don't have to save all these papers."

"Well, Ms. Smarty Pants," she said, "how do I know what I'm looking for if I haven't read about it yet?" She put her fork down on her plate with a loud clatter. "You haven't been talking to Aunt Jean, have you? I knew she wouldn't mind her own business. She's just jealous about all my treasures—"

I was losing control of this situation quickly and had to pull it back if there was ever going to be a chance to look normal to Elaina and the other girls. "No. I would never talk to Auntie Jean. We promised you we wouldn't." My stomach was beginning to churn, but I got up from my chair and put my arm around her to try to get her back on my side. "It's just that some girls wanted to come for a sleepover—you know, for my birthday—and I thought—"

"You thought I was an embarrassment, is that it?" Her

eyes were wet around the corners, and I could see she was going to start crying. She shrugged my arm off. "I'll have you know I work hard for this family just to keep us afloat. No thanks to your deadbeat father, I'm killing myself to keep a roof over all our heads. Maybe other mothers have time to keep their houses spotless because they don't have to work twelve-hour days and then come home to ungrateful children who can't manage to pick up after themselves." She slid her chair back with such force it banged into the sliding glass door. "I don't need to come home to this kind of pressure, Lucy Anne Tompkins." Tears were rolling down her face, and she wasn't doing anything to stop them. "If I'm not good enough for your snotty little girlfriends, then maybe you should find somewhere else to live."

"Maybe I will," I said quietly, staring into my napkin. I knew that was like throwing water on a grease fire, but I couldn't help myself. I was so tired of pretending, of not being good enough.

She inhaled sharply, and put all four legs of the chair back on the ground. "You think so, do you?" she said evenly. "And where would you go? Hmm? Who in the world is going to want an arrogant, whiny, good-for-nothing twelve-year-old baby? Your father?" She laughed. "You really think he wants you ruining his life? His perfect little girlfriend wouldn't let you in their house for a minute."

I could feel my cheeks burning. "Auntie Jean would take me," I said. "She always said she would help us if we needed it."

"Jean?" Mom said with scorn in her voice. "How often have you heard from Aunt Jean?" She took a deep, labored breath. "You really think she's going to want to take you in? Trust me, she doesn't want anything to do with us. Face it, Lucy, I'm all you've got left, so you'd better get used to it." Her face was flushed and she coughed twice.

"I'll run away," I said, staring her down. "Anywhere would be better than here."

"Fine," she said, her voice raspy. She coughed and then inhaled sharply with a gasp. Her breath rattled in her chest as she tried and failed to fill her lungs with air. Mom's arms started flailing and her eyes grew wide with panic as the oxygen failed to come. "Inhaler," she mouthed, pointing to her purse on the floor by the doorway.

"Phil!" I screamed as I dove for her purse. I'd seen Mom's asthma act up before, but I'd never seen an attack this sudden or this severe. I tore through the contents and found the beige inhaler sitting at the bottom. I shook it as I raced back to her place at the table, where she grabbed for it like a lifeline, Phil standing uselessly wide-eyed next to her. After a couple of hits, her breathing was ragged but successful, and the wild panic in her eyes was replaced by weariness. I stood next to her chair, not knowing what to do next, the feelings of hate mixed with guilt for almost killing her. Several long minutes passed as she gained control of her breathing and I held mine, remembering the words that hung between us.

Mom took one last hit on her inhaler and put it in her pocket. She held her hand out to me, and I helped her up out of her chair, her legs still shaking. She braced herself on the table before letting go and testing her balance, her shoulders squared as she stood up and looked me in the eye. "You do what you want," she said and paused for breath. "But I won't be an outcast in my own home." She took a couple of shallow breaths again. "If you walk out that door . . . you'd better be able to make it on your own . . . because you won't be welcome back." She took a few shaky steps out the kitchen door and down the hallway, slamming the door to her room so hard the windows rattled.

I didn't cry or get upset like I usually did—I just felt a numbness that started in my chest and flowed outward with a strange kind of peace. Slowly and carefully, I picked up our plates and carried them both to the sink. At least now I knew what was possible, and I'd never ask her again. I'd start marking down days on the calendar until I could move out on my own and keep my house the way I wanted, and have people over whenever I wanted. It seemed like forever, but what else was I going to do?

"That went well," Phil said, grabbing a dish towel from the drawer next to the sink as I ran water for the dishes. "Anyone walking by probably thought so too."

"Thanks for your support," I said. "She almost died out here, you know. If it hadn't been for her inhaler . . ."

"She'll be fine. Probably sleep until tomorrow, anyway," he said. "I could have told you not to bother." He grabbed a couple of plates that were in the drainer and started slowly rubbing them in circles with the towel. We didn't speak for several long moments. I could feel hot tears beginning to form behind my eyelids as I ran the argument over in my head. She always said it was our fault—that Phil and I couldn't pick up after ourselves, and that's why this place was such a mess. If I ever left so much as one shoe in the hallway, she'd scream and yell like I was the one who stacked up piles of crap in the middle of the living room that were so high you couldn't see around them.

"You know, it wasn't always like this," Phil finally said. He was talking quietly, and I almost didn't hear him over the running water.

I sniffed. "What wasn't like this?"

Phil looked around the kitchen. "This place. The whole house. Mom didn't used to save stuff like she does now," he said. "When Dad was here, everything was clean—almost too clean. Sara and I had to pick up everything, and if we left toys out, Mom would go crazy."

"So Dad was a neat freak?" I was almost afraid to say anything in case he stopped talking.

"No. That's the weird thing. Dad wasn't a slob or anything. He was just regular. Mom was the neat freak."

I let out a laugh so forceful it sounded like a bark. "Right," I said. "Look around, Phil. Mom is the opposite of a neat freak. She's more like some kind of garbage freak."

Phil shook his head. "Seriously," he said. "The whole house was spotless all the time. Mom vacuumed and dusted like every day. She used to say that everything in this house had its place, and it was our job to make sure it got back there." He laughed. "She had this thing about vacuuming—all the lines had to be going in the same direction when you were done, and if you made footprints in the freshly vacuumed carpet, she made you do it again."

I looked around at the piles of stuff that hadn't been touched in years. "I don't remember any of that," I said.

He shrugged. "I guess you were too little." He stopped and looked around too. "It didn't start to get bad until after Dad left." He cleared his throat. "Anyway, we only have to deal with it until we move out. Then she can bury herself in it for all I care."

I turned back to the dishes. "Easy for you to say," I said. "You've only got another year." The thought of being alone with Mom in this house made me nauseous. It seemed like Sara had always had her own apartment and was more like a distant, bossy relative than a real sister—but I wasn't sure I could do it without Phil, even though most of the time he was no help at all. It was just having someone around who understood, even a little bit, what it was like. We weren't one of those families that went around talking about their feelings all the time, but I was sure Phil knew what I was thinking.

"It's not that long," he said. "And besides, I'll probably go someplace close by so I can come and visit all the time. And you can come and stay with me sometimes." He bumped me with his hip. It was probably the closest thing to a hug I'd ever gotten from him. "It's going to be fine. You'll see."

Just then the phone rang, and he ran to get it. I could tell it was a girl by the way his voice got softer and he stretched the cord as far into the dining room as it would go.

I picked the last dish up out of the sink. It was the pink "World's Greatest Mom" mug that she always used for her morning coffee. I stabbed at it with the sponge and tossed it into the drainer without even rinsing it. Maybe I'd get lucky and she'd be right about the germs.

Now, so many years later, I stared at the pink mug in my hand like it was an artifact from a previous civilization. As I threw the mug into the garbage bag with as much force as I could, it was satisfying to hear it break into little pieces.

chapter 9

4:00 p.m.

The smell in the kitchen was giving me a headache, so I decided to take a break from the worst of the mess and go back to the living room. I'd been digging for a while when the shovel hit something at the bottom of one pile that felt solid, not like the papers and clothes that were everywhere else. I leaned against the handle of the shovel and tried to figure out why I couldn't pick up whatever was on the bottom of this pile. It just looked like newspapers and maybe a couple of bags of something else. A McDonald's bag was lying near it, and when I picked it up, the top half tore off of the soggy bottom. The bag must have had food in it when it was set down here however long ago, because whatever it was had liquefied and seeped into the layers of newspaper down below, providing a home and nourishment to a colony of rice-sized maggots. I scrunched up my nose and tossed the remains of the bag into the big green can.

With the shovel, I felt around the edges of the soggy, maggot-infested papers. I put the blade on the very bottom of the pile and tried to lift it, but the pile had been in this spot for so long that the papers were stuck to the carpet. I tried again about halfway up the pile and, with a ripping sound, managed to separate part of it off from the bottom. As it ripped away from the base, the pile of papers flipped into the air, and several of the maggots were flung off the papers and into my face like a larval rain shower.

Raking my fingers through my hair to make sure none landed on me, I felt something cold and wet inside my shirt. I quickly shook it out and watched as one lone maggot landed on the ground, still moving. I ground the disgusting thing into the remains of the carpet with my shoe until it was just a pasty, wet smear.

Spitting and gagging, I ran into my bathroom and went straight to the sink. After splashing cold water over my face and peering intently into the mirror, I was sure with the reasonable part of my brain that there weren't any more maggots on me, but the unreasonable part felt like they were crawling through my scalp and down my neck.

I had come into this part of the job completely unprepared. Tearing off my shirt, I dug around in my drawer for an old turtleneck. There was a bandanna in my sock drawer from when we had Wild West Days at school, so I took it out and tied it around my head to protect my hair from whatever else I was going to find as I cleaned.

Armed with the neck of the shirt pulled up over my mouth, I walked back to the living room. Taking a deep breath, I grabbed the shovel again and tried to pry the stack of newspapers off the carpet. The tip of the shovel dug into the brown fibers as I jammed my foot on the blade to try and work the papers free. Finally, with a wet tearing sound, the small stack broke free of the floor, and I was able to heave it into the trash can. A big patch of the carpet had come up with the papers, and I could see the hardwood floors underneath. I poked at the floor with the metal shovel. Instead of being solid, the wood felt spongy and soft. We definitely couldn't keep the carpet the way it was once the place was cleaned. I wondered how much it would cost to replace an entire floor.

Dark clouds were rolling in as I dragged the bag toward the window, making it seem like dusk even though it was only four o'clock. As I balanced the bag on the sill, I could see the last rays of watery sunshine glowing behind the clouds in the distance as the sun began its roll toward the ocean. The weather didn't usually make much difference to me, because we always kept the curtains closed in the front of the house. I shoved the bag out the window and heard it join the others with a soft sigh.

"Hello?" The voice came from outside. I sucked in my breath and froze. It came again. "Hello?"

Pulling the turtleneck off my face, I stuck my head out the window and tried to manage a normal-looking smile. Mrs. Raj. Even though her house was a pretty good distance from ours, she seemed to think that living next door was an excuse to constantly monitor what we were doing.

"Oh, hello, Mrs. Raj." I sounded remarkably normal, even though I was a little out of breath.

"Doing a bit of early spring cleaning, I see." She stood at the corner of our house where the walkway ended. Her eyes darted to the growing pile of garbage bags, and then back to me.

"Yes, ma'am," I said. I forced a little laugh. "I didn't have anything else to do on vacation, so I thought I'd help Mom out. Just getting rid of a few things."

She pursed her lips and looked at me. "I've heard teenage girls can be rather untidy," she said. "It's nice to see you making a go of it."

Her dog, Tinto, strained at the end of his leash, trying to sniff some of the bags. I hoped she had enough sense to pull him away before he chewed a hole in one.

I'd always begged Mom for a dog, but with her breathing problems, we could never get one. Not that I'd want a dog like Tinto—even calling him a dog was generous. He looked more like a long-haired white rat on a leash and was always barking in that high-pitched yap that could be heard all over the neighborhood.

"Tinto, no!" Mrs. Raj called, pulling him back toward the street. He lifted one flea-bitten leg and peed on the bags as a parting gesture. "Come away from there. I don't want to have to give you another bath today." Mrs. Raj bent down and picked him up, nuzzling him on the nose. "My precious baby."

"Well," I said, giving her a little wave, "have a nice walk. You should probably hurry; it looks like it might rain."

"Yes, we will," she said. She tried to peek around the curtains at my back, so I reached down and held them closed with one hand. "I notice your mother's car hasn't moved from the driveway all day. Is she out of town?"

I kept the smile plastered on my face as my insides were screaming for her to mind her own business. "No. She's home. She's just not feeling well, so she didn't go to work today."

"Oh, I see," she said. She raised her eyebrows. "Is there anything I can do?"

"No, thank you," I said. "We're fine."

"All right, then," she said, and turned like she was going to walk away.

I exhaled, unaware that I had been holding my breath. I started to pull my head back inside the window when she spoke again.

"Oh, Lucy, dear," she called from the sidewalk.

I bumped my head on the bottom of the window as I stuck it outside again. "Yes?" I said brightly through the pain.

Mrs. Raj indicated the growing pile of black trash bags with her hand. "You're not going to leave those bags there, now, are you? You know the town council has rules about compounding garbage that is visible from the street. It would reflect badly on all of us to start a garbage dump on the side of the house."

The whole place is one giant compounded pile of garbage, I wanted to scream. But instead, I smiled sweetly and said, "Only until trash pickup day. I'm going to get tags for extra garbage."

Mrs. Raj sniffed from the sidewalk. "Well, that's very good, dear," she said. "As long as it's gone on trash day. We can't have garbage piling up around our neighborhood, now can we? What would people say?"

"No, we certainly can't," I said. "Have a nice walk, Mrs. Raj. I have to get back to work." I pulled my head in the window and pulled the curtains closed before she had a chance to reply.

"We can't have garbage piling up around our neighborhood," I mimicked as I worked my way back to the living room. No, we certainly could not. Instead, we'd keep it here behind closed doors and live with it every second of our freaking lives.

Mrs. Raj and all those people who were just like her were the reason that I had to get rid of all this crap before anybody could see. Snooty, too-good-for-you busybodies with nothing better to do than to stick their nose in our business. I'll bet Mrs. Raj had been killing herself trying to get in here for years. She was just the type to get invited over to the neighbor's so she could feel that she was so much better than them. Than us. I couldn't let her have the satisfaction.

My phone rang once, so I pulled it out of my front pocket and flipped it open. It was a text from Kaylie asking when I was coming over. I couldn't believe it had gotten so late already. I texted her back that I still had a lot of work to do, trying to stall for time. Anytime I thought about Josh and the look on his face when he asked me to come to the party, I could feel a zing of energy course through my whole body. It would be totally amazing to stand in the crowd watching him play, knowing that he had asked me to come. But it was crazy to leave here, wasn't it? There was no way I could hang out at a party with things the way they were. What if someone came by? And all of that time wasted—it wasn't like I had so much to start with. I would have to come up with something so that Kaylie wouldn't hate me and Josh wouldn't think I was a total loser for not showing up. A few seconds later, the phone rang for real.

"Hey," Kaylie said. "What could you possibly be doing that takes all day?"

"Just some stuff around the house," I answered. "Did you go shopping?"

"Yeah, I got an awesome new bag. What time are you coming over?"

It felt like last night with Josh was a part of another lifetime. I looked around the room and felt the crushing weight of the stuff wash over me. All of a sudden I felt exhausted, like the only thing I wanted was to curl up in bed and sleep for weeks.

"About that," I said. "I don't think I can make it tonight. Something came up." I winced as I said it, knowing she wouldn't let this one go easily. You'd think that all my lying over the years would have made me better at it. You'd think.

There was silence on her end for a long moment. "Something came up? Are you seriously trying to tell me something came up that's more important than seeing Josh play? At a party that he asked you to go to?"

"It's just—"

"No. Way." I could picture Kaylie holding her hand up to the phone. "I don't want to hear any of your excuses." Her voice was getting louder. "I've been planning all day for tonight. You can't let me down like this—you can't let *you* down like this. Josh is totally dying to see you tonight, and you're saying something else came up?" She was really on a roll, so I just waited until it wound down, trying to come up with a good reason why I couldn't go have the best night of my life.

"I can't—"

"At least meet me at Sienna. In twenty. Then you can explain all this to my face."

I knew that if I didn't go to the café she would try to come over here. "Okay—" But the phone went dead.

I wiped my forehead with the back of my arm. I could use a break, and some coffee was definitely in order if I was going to keep at this for much longer. It was almost five o'clock, and I would have to work late into the night—probably all night— to keep making any progress. I had just enough time to change out of my maggot-deflection gear and get over there before she got suspicious.

chapter 10

4:45 p.m.

I ordered my drinks and headed to the bathroom at the back of the café—I'd managed to beat Kaylie here. I knew Josh's work schedule by heart, and luckily he was off on Tuesdays so I didn't have to see face-to-face what I was giving up. I had a feeling that if I looked into those brown eyes, I'd be able to rationalize just about anything.

The bathroom was empty, so I turned on the hot water full blast in the sink and poked at the stream with my finger until it got warm. Once I had the temperature adjusted so that it was just this side of too hot, I ran it over my hands and lower arms, feeling a shiver raise the hairs on the back of my neck as the warmth reached through my skin and into my blood. I stood staring into the running water, enjoying the sensation of hot water cleaning away the maggots and the dirt and the thoughts of everything that had gone on today.

Out of everything else, I missed hot water the most. I had a bathtub in my bathroom, and a couple of times in the last few years I'd warmed up enough hot water in the microwave to take a teeny tiny bath, but it took so long to get bowls of water hot enough that, in the end, it really wasn't worth the effort for five inches of lukewarm water. Showers at the gym were nice, and they never cared that I often stayed in there so long that clouds of steam rolled off my red skin by the time I got out. Maybe we could get a hot tub for the backyard when everything was cleaned out. I'd always wanted a hot tub.

A lady with a bad orange dye job opened the bathroom door and went into a stall, so I just soaped up my hands, rinsed one last time in hot water heaven, and turned off the tap. My hands were red but warm all the way through as I patted them dry with a paper towel and went back out into the busy café.

The frothing sound of the milk steamer was soothing, and it calmed the flutters of panic that kept rising in my throat and threatened to reject the blueberry scone I was picking at. My stomach was starving, but my head wasn't interested. I chewed another piece of scone and looked around. It was somewhere between lunch and dinnertime, and there were a surprising number of people sitting down for their afternoon jolt. Nobody paid attention to me—I just blended in with the rest of the people in the café staring into space and waiting for their drinks. It was amazing that a person could have such a big secret and it didn't show at all.

"Two large vanilla lattes," the girl called, setting my cups on the counter.

Just as I reached for them, Josh walked out from the back room, tying a black apron around his waist. "I'm back if you want to go on break," he said to the cashier. I was frozen between trying to pick up the steaming coffee without being noticed and running away. Damn Kaylie. She must have known he'd be working today, which is why she wanted to meet here.

I grabbed the coffee and tried to turn around quickly, but it didn't work. "Lucy," he said, sounding surprised and (I hoped) happy to see me. "Fueling up before the party tonight? I was on a break, or I'd have gotten you something special." Josh grinned, showing off every one of his perfect white teeth with the small but adorable gap in the middle. He wasn't making this easy, standing there looking like something out of a magazine.

"It's okay. Thanks, though," I said. I pretended to be absorbed in slurping up the little plume of foam that had appeared through the tiny hole in the lid. "Yeah. I'm, uh, meeting Kaylie."

"Here she comes." He nodded toward the front doors.

Kaylie walked in with the phone to her ear, talking loudly to someone, but she snapped it shut as soon as she saw us. "Good," she said. "You're here. I guess you've told him already?"

Josh tilted his head and looked at me. "Told me what?"

I willed more people to show up and desperately need caffeine, but it looked like everyone in town was taken care of for the moment. I took a sip of the hot latte. "Mmm. Maybe later. You're busy." I made a move toward an empty table, but Kaylie grabbed my arm and held me there.

"Lucy has decided that she can't come tonight, after all," Kaylie said to Josh. "Something has 'come up.'" She made little quotation marks in the air with her fingers.

It was hard to read Josh's reaction. Even though I knew that there was no way I could show up at the party, I wanted him to look at least a little disappointed.

"You sure? We've been working on this new song, and I really wanted you to hear it." I had to admit, he looked pretty sincere.

"Yeah," I said. "I'm sorry, I really can't." Looking into his eyes was like looking directly at the sun—do it too long and you could go blind. I stared down at the scuffs on my Converse. "Next time, maybe?"

"Sure," he said. He reached across the counter, but just then the bells on the front door rang and three women walked in. Josh looked like he wanted to say something else, but instead he turned to the customers. "Good afternoon. What can I get for you?" As he ignored me and became all businesslike, I started to realize what had just happened. Josh had asked me out once, and chances were, he wasn't going to do it again.

Kaylie ordered a coffee and headed for an open table. "Come. Sit."

"I really do have to—"

Kaylie kicked the chair under the table so it scooted in my direction. "Sit. You at least owe me that for bailing."

So I sat. Kaylie had been my best friend since the start of school this year—longer than I'd ever been best friends with anyone before. She didn't ask a lot of questions and always believed my answers, which to me were important qualities for a best friend. I couldn't afford to blow it, especially now. After what happened to my last "best friend," I swore I'd never let it happen again.

I'd always been careful before. Whenever I got picked up at the house, I made sure to meet people out front or on the curb. I spent a lot of time waiting outside, but it was worth not having to explain why they couldn't come in. I should have been waiting at the end of the driveway for Elaina and her mom to pick me up that day. Even though I'd never been able to pull off the slumber party, she and a couple of girls in my class still seemed interested in hanging out with me. I'd fooled myself into thinking they liked me. Instead of waiting at the curb that day, I was in the bathroom trying to get one side of my hair to lie flat like it was supposed to. Once I noticed what time it was, it was too late. Elaina was knocking on the front door before I could even get down the hall. I stood on the other side of the door with my heart racing, trying to figure out what I was going to do.

"Hey, Elaina," I yelled through the door. "I'll be out in a sec. I'll meet you down at the car."

"Okay," she yelled back.

I took a deep breath. Close calls always freaked me out. I stood on my side of the door for two whole minutes just to make sure, but when I opened it, Elaina was standing on the other side. Even worse, she slid into the doorway before I could pull it shut.

"You know what?" she said. "I really need to . . ." Her words tapered off as she took a look around the parts of the house that she could see. "I, um, really need to pee." She looked directly at me with a funny smirk on her face. "Can I use your bathroom?"

"I, uh, it's broken," I said, knowing in the pit of my stomach that it was already too late. Our hallway bathroom was covered in mildew, and the shower was filled with papers and bags of clothes, but technically it still worked. She'd have to push her way through the rest of the house to get there, though, and there was no way I was going to make this worse.

"Broken?" Elaina asked, staring at the piles of newspapers that lined the hallway. "How does a bathroom get broken?"

"We're remodeling." I tried to block her way into the house, but just then Mom came around the corner and stopped in her tracks at the sight of Elaina on the wrong side of the door.

Her hands flew to her hair, as if having a few hairs out of place was the worst thing we had going. "Oh, hello, dear," she said. Her voice was shaking and her eyes were darting around the room. "Are you girls going out?"

"I was just telling Elaina that she can't use the bathroom. Because of the remodel." I sent Mom messages with my eyes to please, please go along with me. She hated lying, but she hated having people in the house even more.

Mom couldn't keep her hands still, and they flew around her body like they were possessed. She reached out to touch some of the newspapers and to smooth the cover of a *National Geographic* that had gotten bent, but until she opened her mouth, I wasn't sure what she would do. "Right. The remodel." I was afraid Elaina would see my relief. For once, Mom was on my side. She looked directly at Elaina for the first time. "Perhaps we can go next door and ask Mrs. Raj if you can use hers?"

Elaina took one last look around, memorizing the piles of junk that reached almost to the ceiling. "That's okay," she said. "I guess I can wait."

I grabbed my bag, and all three of us slipped out of the house. I didn't dare look at Elaina, but Mom cut her eyes at me like she'd never been so angry in her life. I knew she'd blame me for letting Elaina in on purpose, even though I spent all my time trying to keep people away. I was glad I was going out, because then maybe she'd cool off by the time I got home.

Mom followed us down the driveway and plastered on a normal-looking smile as she waved to Elaina's mom in the driver's seat. "Hi, Victoria," she said as she reached the van. "Thanks so much for taking Lucy with you."

"Oh, it's no trouble at all," Elaina's mom said.

I pulled the back door open and strapped myself into the van. I tried to stare straight ahead and listen to their conversation, but I couldn't stop thinking about what Elaina had seen. I started to breathe faster and had to will myself to calm down. Maybe it wouldn't be as bad as I thought. Maybe Elaina would just think the place was a little messy, is all.

After what seemed like an hour and a half, Mom stepped back from the van with a wave. "All set?" Elaina's mom asked.

"Yup," Elaina said as the van pulled away from the curb. She watched out the front window as her mother drove, but kept sneaking glances back at me as she talked. I swear I saw her nose wrinkle just a little. That whole afternoon, Elaina seemed normal but distant. There was no way I was going to bring it up, so we just acted like nothing had happened, and I'd hoped that was the end of it. I found out at school on Monday that it was nowhere near the end of it.

The balled-up piece of notebook paper hit me in the back of the head to the sound of giggling from the back of the room. It landed near my right foot, so I bent down to pick it up. As quietly as I could, I straightened it out in my lap so that I could see the cartoon of what was probably supposed to be me, with boogers dripping down my face and flies buzzing around me. I was sitting on top of a mountain of junk and underneath the whole thing were the words "Garbage Girl" written in big black marker.

I looked toward the back of the room, but everyone was staring at their desks, pretending to write in their journals. It could have been anyone, really—aside from Elaina, I didn't have any real friends. Maybe now I didn't have any friends at all.

"Lucy, do you have something to share?" The voice from the front of the room echoed in the stillness.

"No, Sister," I said, and tucked the disgusting drawing away in my notebook.

To my left, Curtis Swanson coughed loudly, but I swear I heard the words "Garbage Girl" come out of his mouth. Over the next couple of weeks, I was going to hear it a lot. Elaina avoided me like I stunk, and I got notes and drawings stuffed in my locker almost every day. I finally told Phil about it after I'd said I had a stomachache and stayed home from school for three straight days. For once he wasn't a jerk—he was the sympathetic brother I'd always wanted sticking up for me. Now that he was older, Mom treated him more like another adult. Maybe she knew he was on his way out.

I don't know how he did it, but Phil got Mom to let me go to public school right after that. She said it was because Catholic school was too expensive, but communication wasn't a strong point in our family. I was just glad the whole "Garbage Girl" episode hadn't followed me this far. Yet.

I glanced back at the front counter where Josh was helping some more customers. He wasn't even looking in my direction. I'd missed my chance and he'd already moved on. Probably relieved that I'd changed my mind.

Kaylie picked up her coffee and walked back to the table, squinting at the display on her phone, trying to read a text. "So it looks like I'm meeting Vanessa at nine—are you sure you can't come?"

I nodded quickly and took another sip of coffee.

"I'm sorry I got all mad at you on the phone. Is it your mom's head again?" she asked. She looked sympathetic, but that was probably because she had Vanessa as backup. Maybe Kaylie was moving on too.

"Yeah," I managed, grateful that she'd remembered my lie. Over the past couple of years, I'd told people that Mom had a brain tumor, multiple sclerosis, epilepsy, Alzheimer's, kidney failure, and irritable bowel syndrome as reasons for why I couldn't do something or have them over. I always felt a little guilty saying it, like I was jinxing Mom somehow. Maybe I was.

"I thought the brain surgery was supposed to cure the seizures," she said.

"It will," I said. "But the doctors said it might take up to a year. She's . . . she's not doing so good right now."

"That sucks," she said. She glanced up at the counter where I didn't dare look again. "I just think Josh would be so good for you, you know? You need to have a little more fun in your life. You're always so serious."

I couldn't answer her. I just looked down and studied my fingernails.

"I mean, I know you don't let guys rule your life and everything," she said. "And you don't care what people think about you. But still."

All I could do was look at her and nod at this totally distorted image of me that she seemed to have. I'd love to let guys rule my life, if my life was normal. The fact that she thought my hiding from the world was some display of maturity was actually a little sad.

"Are you okay?" Kaylie asked. She leaned her face in closer to mine. "You look funny."

I plastered a smile on my face. "Yeah, I'm fine."

"Maybe later I could come and help you, so that you could get out of there," she said. "You never let me come over to help, even though you're all alone with her."

As she said that, the backs of my eyes started stinging, like I was going to start bawling. The worst part was there was *nobody* who could help me—nobody that I could even tell. Dad had made it clear that sending money every month was about as much involvement as he wanted with us, and all he'd do was tell me to call 911. Or worse, call them for me. He'd probably be relieved if I could persuade Phil to move back in with me afterward so that he wouldn't have to deal with it, but I wasn't convinced that Phil would see things my way. What if I told him what had happened and he called the police? Sara would definitely *not* see things my way and would have the house surrounded by flashing lights in no time. I had effectively been an orphan for the past eight hours or so, and I had to keep the biggest secret of my life all to myself.

"No. Thanks," I said. I rubbed my eyes with the palms of my hands. Kaylie looked at me like she wanted me to say more. "Why . . . why do you even bother?" I finally asked.

"Bother with what?" Kaylie looked genuinely confused.

I was sure that my nose was bright red by now and that I looked even more pathetic than usual. Luckily, nobody around seemed to be listening. "With me," I said quietly, wiping my nose to make sure there was nothing dripping. "You've got Vanessa and all of your other friends. I just wreck your plans."

She sat back in her chair. "Are you serious?"

I didn't say anything else. I knew that I sounded like a whiny pain in the neck, but it might be easier if I just got rid of everyone—all two of them—in one quick afternoon. Maybe after all this was over I could make new friends—have a boyfriend, even, but things were getting too complicated right now.

"First of all," Kaylie said, "you don't wreck everything. Okay, yeah, you bail on me sometimes, but you've got a lot going on. Do you remember art class last year?"

Of course I did. Kaylie sat at the next table while my partner was the annoying Miles Harris, pitcher for the baseball team and all-around idiot who threatened to ruin my favorite class. I tried to ignore him, and all the girls in the class who would always find excuses to come by our table, by drawing pictures of the house I was going to design someday. Kaylie started talking to me toward the end of the year, first asking to borrow a pen or some paper and later asking me to tag along with her when she went out on the weekends.

"You were the only one who wasn't dying to sit next to Miles—you even seemed irritated by him. You'd just sit there drawing these really amazing pictures, and your projects were always so much better than mine. It was like you had more important things to deal with than the hottie sitting next to you. I wanted to find out what your secret was." She laughed.

If Kaylie ever did find out the real secret, she wouldn't think it was so funny. "I don't have a secret," I lied.

"Yes, you do," she said. I felt a momentary flutter of dread, but I knew she wasn't anywhere near the truth. "Your secret is that you really *don't* care about all the stuff that goes on in school. You're somehow removed from it all." She sat forward again. "Which is why this whole Josh thing is so awesome. I just don't want you to walk away from him."

"I'm not," I said. "It's just that tonight . . . I can't come tonight." I didn't want to tell her how much I really did care about what Josh thought and what he was doing. And who he was doing it with. Leaving yourself vulnerable was the quickest way to have anything good taken away from you. If I'd learned anything from Mom, it was that.

"Well, I'll totally keep an eye on him for you," she said. "I'm not going to let him get away, in spite of you."

I managed a smile. "Thanks, Kay," I said. I tossed back the last of the coffee in my cup. "I really do have to head back," I said, and stood up.

Kaylie sighed. "If you say so. Do you want me to walk with you?"

"No, it's cool. I have to stop at Safeway."

She leaned over the table and gave me a hug. "I'll call you if anything good happens."

I nodded and picked up the second cup of coffee I'd ordered.

"Didn't you just have coffee?" she asked.

"Yeah," I said. "This one's for Mom. I promised her I'd bring some back with me." The one thing I didn't have set up in my room was a coffee maker, and I was going to need all the help I could get if I was going to keep working until late at night.

"Don't let my mom hear you say that," she said. "She already thinks you're the perfect daughter. She's always joking that she'd like to adopt you and have you come live with us."

I could never tell Kaylie how perfect that would be. As much as I wanted to grow up and be on my own, I wished for someone to take care of me so I wouldn't have to worry all the time. I thought of my mother's sheet-covered body lying in the hallway at that very second. Every time I started to feel guilty, I had to remind myself that I was doing it for all of us. But that still didn't change the fact that Mom was dead, and I was sitting here talking and drinking coffee. I wondered what Kaylie's mom would think about that. "Don't worry," I said. "I'm not so perfect."

Josh was busy up front, so I just walked out the door without another word. It was probably best this way. It felt like a solid lead ball was sitting in the pit of my stomach. I couldn't stand thinking about him at the party tonight. As much as I liked to think I was special, there would be so many girls there, he wouldn't even notice I was missing. He'd probably be going out with someone else by the time vacation was over.

Walking home, I carried a bag from the grocery store and balanced the coffee in one hand, hoping that and some egg rolls from the deli would keep me at least until tomorrow. I'd really wanted fried rice, but as I bent down to look at it in the deli case, all I could think of was the maggot I'd brushed out of my shirt earlier. As much as it used to be my favorite food, thanks to one lone, preadolescent fly, fried rice was probably lost to me forever. I'd also loaded up on more rubber gloves and those paper face masks that supposedly protect you from chemicals and irritants. We should probably have been living in these all along.

The walk was short, but it felt good to be out in the cold air. I zipped my jacket up to my chin so only the top of my head and my face were freezing. It was starting to get dark, and most of the houses still had their Christmas lights on outside, which made the cold darkness seem not so bad. Like it had a purpose, even.

As I walked up our street, I looked in the windows of the houses I passed. I could see people sitting down to dinner, or the blue glow on the walls from the TV.

The Callans a few houses down had their curtains open, and I could see the Christmas tree all lit up by the window. I was sure Mrs. Callan would be in the kitchen cooking, waiting for Mr. Callan to come home. Hanging out in their house had made me realize that not everyone had parents who loved their stuff more than they loved their kids.

The air smelled like a campfire, and I thought about how nice it would be to sit by a warm fire on such a cold night. Maybe we could get the fireplace working again once everything was done. Phil and I would keep a big stack of wood on the porch and feed it to the fire every time it started to die. Maybe we could have regular movie nights in the winter, where we'd invite people over, make popcorn, and sit in front of the fire, watching movies with all the lights off. At this point I should have probably stopped with the "maybes" and "what-ifs," but whenever the now got bad, thinking about the future always made me feel better.

chapter 11

5:30 p.m.

"Lucy!"

I stopped dragging the green bin across the dining room and listened. It was high and faint, but it was definitely my name. The hairs on the back of my neck stood up, and my heart beat faster.

I pulled down my face mask. "Mom?" I whispered cautiously, and immediately felt ridiculous. I had to be hearing things. Since I'd only put on lights in the dining room, it was pitch black in the rest of the house now—and starting to get a little creepy, if I let myself think about it. I slowly tiptoed out of the dining room and down the hall, trying to calm myself. Mom was definitely dead the last time I looked. No amount of moving her stuff around and looking in forbidden boxes would turn her into an angry ghost. At least, that's what I hoped.

I got to the back hallway and flicked on the overhead light. The sheet was still there. I swallowed hard and tried to reason with myself. This was crazy. Whatever I was hearing, it definitely wasn't Mom calling me. At least not from the hallway.

I walked back to the dining room and started moving boxes again. As I was stuffing some newspapers in a garbage bag, I heard it again. A small voice calling my name.

"Stop it!" I yelled out loud this time. I was starting to panic when movement at the window caught my eye. Before I could react, the curtains parted, and TJ stuck his head through them.

"Hey!" he said. "Didn't you hear me calling you?"

"Man, TJ," I said. My knees wobbled with relief, and I felt like I had to sit down. "You scared the crap out of me."

"Did I?" he said, not looking ashamed. "I wasn't sneaking up on you or anything. I yelled and stuff." He scrunched up his nose and looked around. "What stinks?"

I ignored that last statement and crossed the room until I was standing above him at the window. "What are you doing out there?" I peeked out the window and saw him standing on the stack of plastic bags. Only TJ wouldn't think to ask what a giant stack of plastic bags was doing along the side of the house.

He looked around the room. "Are you moving or something? Who's going to babysit me when Mom goes out?"

"Knock it off," I said. "We're not moving. I told you, I'm just cleaning up some stuff."

"Cool." TJ looked behind him. "Can I come in?"

"No!" I answered just a little too quickly. "You can't come in. It's not a good idea. You said yourself it stinks in here."

"I didn't mean it. Come on," he said. "I can help. Plus, you said you'd see if you could find some of Phil's stuff for me to go through."

I hesitated just long enough for him to see the crack in my resolve. TJ was one of those kids that spent his free time wandering the neighborhood waiting for someone to ask him to come over. Whatever the reason, he hated being home—a feeling I understood more than anyone else on the block. Plus, he was a pretty good kid.

"It's freezing out here," he said. "Can't I just come in for a little bit?"

Even though I willed myself not to look back toward the hallway, I could feel my thoughts wandering in that direction. It was dark out now, and even though I could still hear the music from the kitchen, I had to admit it would be nice having another living body in the house. How much could a kid figure out, anyway?

"Shouldn't you be in bed or something?" I asked.

"It's not even six o'clock," he said. "Mom lets me stay up until nine during vacations. She's having that weird guy from work over for dinner, so I had to get out of there." TJ's mom had been divorced for a couple of years and seemed to go out with a new boyfriend every week. TJ didn't seem to like it, but she kept the babysitting jobs coming, so it wasn't a problem as far as I was concerned.

I looked around. It was crazy to let TJ in. Nobody had been in here in years, and I was just going to let him climb through the window? I thought about how quiet and a little creepy it was without him here but what a huge risk I'd be taking.

"If I do let you in, you have to promise me that you'll stay in this room."

"I promise," he said, not even asking why. I could hear his feet kicking and scraping at the wood siding on the house. He stopped and looked up at me. "A little help?"

I reached down and grabbed the belt loops on the back of

his pants and swung him into the room. He reached over to close the window, but I stopped him. "No, leave it open."

"It's freezing out there. Why do you want it open?"

"I, uh . . ." I tried to think of a good reason why I needed the window open in the middle of winter. "The garbage disposal backed up and I'm trying to get the smell out."

"My mom just uses air freshener," he said, taking a good look around the room. "Wow, you guys have a lot of stuff. This is totally cool."

"Ya think?" I said. "Well, I'm trying to get rid of stuff we don't need. Which is pretty much all of it."

"I'll take it." TJ started poking his finger in some of the cardboard boxes that were stacked against the wall.

I grabbed his hand and looked him in the eye. "What I want you to do is help me grab all of the green plastic bins in this room and the living room over there and we're going to stack them up against the wall. Under no circumstances are you to go in any other room. You will be banned forever if you do."

"Why?" he asked.

"Because I said so."

"Okay, but why?"

"I don't want you to get hurt," I said, knowing it was a lame answer.

TJ shrugged and bundled his jacket tighter. "Can you turn the heat on?" he asked. "It's just as freezing in here as it is outside."

"Yeah, well," I said, "we're trying to save energy, so I can't do that right now."

"You're going to wake up dead then," he said. "'Cause you're going to freeze to death."

If he only knew.

He poked at one of the green plastic bins. "So what is all this stuff, anyway?"

"I don't really know," I said. "It's mostly my mom's."

He looked at the growing wall of green bins and piles of belongings in both the dining room and living room. "Well, she must be rich, because I've never seen anyone with so much stuff before."

Rich. That was hilarious. "I don't know about rich," I said. "She just never gets rid of anything." I started moving boxes off some bins that were stacked along one window.

"Not anything?"

"Nope. Not anything." I stacked the boxes on top of some others in the middle of the room and started dragging one of the bins toward our growing stack.

"How about books that you guys have already read?"

I pointed to the overflowing bookcase in the front hallway. If I read one book every day for two years, I'd never get through them all. "Nope."

"How about a snotty-nose tissue that someone who has the worst cold in the world has blown their nose in until it was dripping with boogers?"

I stopped to think for a minute. "Well, she might throw that away," I said. "But if someone was working on an art project that could incorporate a snotty, boogery nose tissue, then she would keep it in a bag somewhere until she could give it to them."

"Ewww!" TJ said. Then he started laughing. "That is so gross. What about a whole sculpture made with snotty-nose rags, belly button lint, and earwax?" He started laughing so hard that he bent over double and had to sit down on one of the bins.

As I watched him laugh, I started smiling too. Somewhere in this mess I just might find a bag full of snotty tissue, belly button lint, and earwax. I wouldn't put it past her. It was weird telling all this to TJ. None of us ever talked about it outside of the house, but for some reason he felt safe. Even if he said anything to his mom, she wouldn't believe him. Nobody would believe that the stories he was telling about our garbage pit were true. No one would choose to live like this.

"Okay, okay," I said. I clapped my hands. "Come help me drag this bin over to those. This one is heavy, so be careful."

He grabbed the front handle and I grabbed the back, and together we picked the bin up just a few inches off the floor and crabwalked it over to the others. "What's in here?" TJ asked, and before I could stop him, he pulled the lid off. "Oh, cool!"

I peeked over the edge and was relieved to see it was just a pile of old books she must have had a greater plan for.

TJ picked one up and looked at the spine. "What are they? They all look the same."

I grabbed one and recognized it right away because we had another set buried in a bookcase in the living room. "They're encyclopedias."

He looked at me blankly.

"You know, books people used to use if they needed to find out about something. Kind of like Google, only in real life." I showed him the side of the book I was holding. "See, this one has everything that starts with *V*. I used to read these when I was little, like they were regular books."

He picked up another volume and flipped through it. "Can I keep them?" He shuffled through the books in the box and pulled out two. "I'll take *T* and *J*." He stuck his hand back in and pulled out another one. "And *L* too. *L* for Lucy."

"Okay, but that's it," I said. "We'll ask your mom about the rest later."

As I lifted a small mountain of shoeboxes and started to step on them so they would fit into the bag better, I spotted the heavy brass corners and battered black leather of the trunk that I hadn't seen for years. Grandma had died before I was born, and Mom kept Grandma's special stuff in this trunk. If Mom and I were alone at night, she would sometimes let me sit with her and look at the yellowing bonnets and tiny lace shoes Grandma had saved from when Mom was a baby. I'd always wanted to put the clothes on my dolls, but Mom said they were too old to play with. The trunk opened with a loud creak that got TJ's attention across the room.

"What is it?" He came and knelt down by the trunk.

"Some of my grandma's stuff," I said. The bonnets and booties were still carefully folded on top.

"Are you going to keep it?"

I nodded. "I think I should."

Stacked in the corner was a set of gold-rimmed plates with pink flowers on them. Mom always said we would use these plates sometime when the occasion was special enough. As far as I knew, there had never been an occasion special enough. I took one finger and ran it through the thick coat of dust that had formed on the small top plate. In three short moves I made two eyes and a frowning mouth. Poor, lonely plates. Once this stuff was cleaned up, maybe I'd keep the plates. Except that when I was in charge, we'd use them every day.

TJ stuck his head in the trunk. "It smells like old people in here," he said. He reached in and pulled out something from the bottom. "Was your grandma in the Olympics or something?"

I squinted at what he had in his hand. "Not that I know of."

"Well, here's a gold medal from somewhere." He handed me a heavy medal that hung on a faded red, white, and blue ribbon.

I turned it over. On the back was engraved: *First Place, Central Conservatory Piano Competition.* I shrugged. "I never met my grandma. She must have been a good piano player."

TJ was digging in the trunk again, and I was afraid he was going to wreck something. I wanted to put the whole thing aside until I had time to go through it piece by piece. Mom never talked very much about growing up—her stories never started with "When I was a kid" like a lot of other parents.

"Let's leave this alone," I said. "I'll go through it later." I reached for the baby clothes to put them back in the top of the trunk.

"What's a 'prodigy'?" TJ asked.

I looked over his shoulder at the yellowed newspaper he was reading. "It's a little kid who is really smart or really good at something."

"Well, this little kid is really good at the piano," he said, pointing to a photo of a small girl seated on a piano bench, her shiny patent leather shoes dangling above the floor. "Is that your grandma?"

"Let me see." I took the paper and looked more closely.

The caption under the photo read: "Local piano prodigy little Joanna Coles can barely reach the keys, but she performed like a professional at the Central Conservatory of Music Piano Competition, where she beat out all comers to win first prize."

"Huh. It's my mom." I looked at the date on the paper. "She would have been about nine years old."

TJ hoisted a big black leather book onto his lap. The pages creaked and the plastic sleeves stuck together as he opened it. "Looks like she won a lot of stuff."

We quietly flipped through the pages that showed Mom's progress from a cute little girl whose feet didn't touch the floor to a beautiful teenager seated elegantly in front of a white baby grand piano in a sleeveless ball gown. Her neck was long, and she gazed straight into the camera, as though daring anyone to doubt her talent.

The newspaper clippings showed win after win at local and even national piano competitions—photos of Mom accepting medals and trophies of all sizes. The book was only half full, and the clippings stopped abruptly in 1970. The rest of the shiny, black pages were blank. Mom would have been about seventeen.

TJ shut the book. "Did she quit?"

I felt like I had been looking at pictures of someone I'd never met. Why hadn't she ever shown me any of this before? Why did she stop playing? She never let me dig in the trunk, and now I knew why. I realized with a jolt that I'd never get these answers. "I don't know," I finally said to TJ.

"You should ask her." He stood up and looked around the room.

I put the book on top of the baby clothes and carefully shut the trunk. "Yeah, I should." There were so many things I'd never know the answers to now. "Enough of this. You go finish up over by that wall, and I'll take care of these things." I needed something to distract me. Something that would take my mind off the photos and the clippings and the trophies that had never made it into this part of Mom's life. I wondered what had happened to that girl who looked like she could win anything, to turn her into someone who wouldn't even answer the front door.

chapter 12

6:00 p.m.

"Oh yuck!"

"What?" I prayed there weren't any maggots, because I wasn't sure how I would explain those away. High school science experiment? Suburban 4-H?

"This box is all soggy and gross," TJ said. He had the flaps open and was picking out mildewed bits of paper that disintegrated and fell heavily back into the box as he held them up.

"It's okay," I said. "Just shove everything into this garbage bag."

"Hey, Lucy, this looks good," he said. "Can I keep it?"

I looked over to see him holding up a plastic bag containing Teddy B., the brown gingham teddy bear I'd made by hand in third grade. I walked over to take a better look at the box.

"Did your mom make it?" TJ asked.

"No," I said. "I did. It was a Girl Scout project—I even got my sewing badge for doing it. My mom used to make quilts a long time ago—she was a really good sewer, and she showed me what to do."

I squeezed the bear's tummy and looked at the small brown stitches that ran the length of his side, thinking about the nights Mom and I had sat with our heads bent over the effort of making the stitches that held him together as tiny and uniform as possible.

"Here," Mom had said softly, taking the floppy, unstuffed bear from my lap. "Just put the needle in a little ways, like this." I could feel the warmth of her body straight from the shower, and her wet hair tickled my chin as she bent over our work. We sat in a cleared space on the living room couch, piles of newspapers and scraps of quilting fabric surrounding the small, folding TV tray that held our supplies. "You want to try?"

She handed the brown fabric back to me, the needle sticking up at an angle. "Just put your finger behind the fabric where you want the stitch to go," Mom said, watching my fingers as I worked. Beside her tight, tiny stitches, mine looked like something that would have held Frankenstein's monster together. "That's good. Just try to get them a little bit closer together."

I tried to concentrate even harder, wanting my stitches to match hers so she'd be proud of me. "You mean like th—? Ow!" I cried, the sharp end of the needle making a searing stab at my finger.

"Oh, let me see," Mom said, pulling my finger into her lap. She dabbed at it with the edge of her shirt. "I think you'll live." Mom smiled at me. "Congratulations. You are now an official member of the top secret quilting society."

I dabbed at the mark in the middle of my finger. "What's that?" I was mad that I'd done something so stupid and wrecked what we were doing.

"Hold on a minute," Mom said, and jumped up to rummage

in the big tote bag she kept next to the recliner. "I know it's in here somewhere." She pawed through material and thread, and dug way down to the bottom. "Aha! I knew I'd seen it," she said, and held out something small and round.

I took it and held it up to the dim light. It was like a tiny metal hat with dents all over the top and a pretty painted blue picture of windmills all around the base. "What is it?"

"Lucy Tompkins! Are you telling me that you don't know a thimble when you see one?"

I shrugged, trying to keep her in a good mood. I held it back out to her. "It's pretty."

Mom laughed. "It is pretty," she said, and took it back to look it over more carefully. "It was my mother's, and she gave it to me when she taught me to sew. You put it on your finger like this." She popped it on the end of her pointer finger. "And then the needles won't stick you."

I gave her a small smile. "Cool."

She held up my injured finger and set the little thimble on the end. "Now it's yours," she said.

It took a little while to get used to wearing it, but I didn't poke myself again.

I hadn't thought of that thimble in years. Somewhere, in some box or bag or green bin, was an antique thimble that I'd probably never see again.

TJ held out his hand for the bear. "So, do I get to keep him?"

I held Teddy B. a little tighter. He was physical proof that things hadn't always been this bad. "You know what, T? Let's find something else for you to keep. I think I'm going to hang on to this for a while."

"Fine," he said, and started grabbing things out of the box again.

I tucked Teddy B. into the front of my jacket and bent down to see what else was in the box. On one side my name was written in black marker that flowed with my mother's handwriting.

Taking a handful of soggy papers out of the box, I could see they were a mix of kindergarten drawings, report cards, and those meaningless paper certificates you get for completing a reading program or passing Tadpole swim lessons at the Y. Mom must have put everything in here to save for when I got older. And now everything was destroyed. She had fifty plastic bins in this house full of pristine crap—why couldn't she actually put something meaningful in them? Like a special silver and blue thimble? Or my childhood?

I was scraping the pieces of cardboard off the soggy rug when I heard a yelp and a crash, as a large stack of books and papers toppled to the floor. "TJ! Are you okay?" I jumped up and ran over to him.

He was sitting on the floor surrounded by an avalanche of books. "I'm okay," he said, but I could tell by the wetness around the edges of his eyes it hurt more than he let on. "I'm sorry." He frantically tried to pick up some of the books. "I didn't mean it, really. It was just an accident . . . I turned around and my shoulder hit the stack and—"

I remembered saying those exact words so many times to Mom as she screamed at me to be careful. In her world, there was no such thing as an accident, just people who didn't pay enough attention. I bent down and grabbed TJ's face in my hands. "It's not your fault, okay?" That's what I always wanted someone to say to me. "Come on, let me feel where the books got you," I said. Even though it had just happened, I could feel the start of a big bump on his head behind his right ear. "No blood," I said. "But I think your mom should take a look." I stood up and held my hand out for him.

"No," he whined. "I don't want to go. We're not done yet."

"Yeah, I know," I said. "But if I send you home broken, your mom's going to be really mad at me. If I find anything cool, I'll put it in a pile for you."

TJ touched one finger to the growing lump on his head. "You won't even know what's cool," he grumbled. "You'll probably throw out good stuff that I want to keep."

"I know what you like, don't worry about it. You need ice on that, so let's go. I'll walk you home."

We picked our way back through the dining room and into the front hallway. "Hold on, I need my books," he said, and picked them up off the floor. "Don't forget to save the other ones."

"They're yours," I said. We opened the door and stepped out into the biting air. It was unusually cold, for which I was undeniably grateful. We hurried across the street to TJ's house, his Christmas tree still sparkling in the window.

His steps slowed as we approached the porch. "*He's* still here," he said. "That's his ugly green car. He used to go home early, like right after dinner, and now they sit around watching TV and stuff."

"You don't like him?" I asked.

TJ shrugged as much as he could with his arms wrapped around three huge encyclopedias. "He's okay. He's always trying to get me to go and play ball with him. I keep telling him I hate playing ball, but he won't listen. Plus, Mom's always busy now—not like she used to be."

I nodded, not pushing it any further. I knew how hard it was not feeling welcome in your own house.

The door was locked, so I rang the bell as TJ stood on the bottom step. His mom opened it with a glass of wine in her hand. "Oh hi, Lucy," she said. "Was TJ with you? I thought he'd gone down to the Callans' house to watch TV."

"Well, he's been helping me move some things around. He said you wouldn't mind."

"Of course not," she said, smiling at me. "I just hope he wasn't a bother."

"No, he was fine," I said. "But some books fell and hit him in the head. I think he might need some ice." I grabbed TJ's arm and guided him up the stairs.

His mom ruffled his hair and inspected the spot he showed her. "It looks okay, but you're right, it probably does need ice." She pulled back and looked into his face. "So what were you doing over there that caused books to fall on your head? I hope you weren't running around and making trouble."

"Oh no," I said quickly, "it's not his fault. The books . . . they were where they shouldn't have been, and he was just walking by them. Really, he didn't do anything wrong."

"If you say so," she said. "I'd hate to think of him over there making a mess."

I looked at TJ, but he didn't seem to think that was funny. Maybe it didn't look all that weird to him. Kids were sometimes strange that way. "No, really," I said. "He was great. I hope his head is okay."

"I'm sure he'll be fine. TJ, say thanks to Lucy for putting up with you."

"Thanks, Lucy," he said. "Don't forget about my stuff." He held his books up to his mom. "They have so much cool stuff over there. Lucy gave me these encyclopses so I can learn about everything that begins with these letters."

"Wow," she said. "You got some real treasures." She backed into the house. "Thanks again for having him."

"No problem," I said.

As the door closed, I could hear TJ talking a mile a minute. "They've got a whole box of these books, and Lucy said I could have them all. Can I keep them in my room?"

I stood on the porch for just a minute, looking through the filmy curtains at the colored lights twinkling on the Christmas tree branches, before I turned and walked down the steps to my house.

As I reached the end of TJ's driveway, my heart started pounding, and I broke into a run. Our house was directly across the street from theirs, but it had never looked so far away. Especially with Sara's car parked in our driveway.

chapter 13

6:30 p.m.

I stuck my foot out to stop the front door from shutting and tried not to look like I'd been running. Sara was still standing in the hallway, so I knew she hadn't seen anything.

"Hey," I said, hoping the panic I was feeling was well hidden. Unlike Phil, who had to be dragged back, Sara came over a couple of times a week—not because she cared about me, but because she wanted to make sure she was still Mom's favorite. "What're you doing here?"

"It's still my house too, in case you forgot," she said, sounding more like Mom every day. "Where were you? The door wasn't even locked. Anybody could have walked right in." As far as I was concerned, anybody did.

"Oh, I just had to run across the street for a minute. Babysitting stuff."

Sara nodded slowly, like she was trying to decide if I was telling the truth. "Well, I called Mom at work to see if she wanted to meet up for dinner, but they said she was sick."

I nodded. "Yeah. Some sort of nasty flu thing." I coughed a little for emphasis. "You should probably get out of here before you catch it. I'm sure we're contagious."

She held up a shopping bag. "I brought over some Chinese to make her feel better." Sara stepped back and looked into the living room, but Mom's recliner was empty. "Where is she?"

I leaned to the side to block her access to the kitchen. I could feel the thoughts whirling through my head as I tried to come up with something that would get her out of here as quickly as possible. If Sara thought that something was going on, she'd call 911 in a second. Sara went along with Mom's philosophy that there was nothing wrong with the house that a little straightening wouldn't fix. Mom wasn't one of those hoarders, she was a saver—saving the planet one stack of newspapers at a time. Now that everything was "eco" and "green," they had even more backup. It was like she wasn't even standing in the same house that I was.

"Uh, Mom's in my room," I heard myself say. "She was so sick I let her sleep in my room all day."

"Well, I'll just stick my head in and make sure she's okay," she said. She took a few steps toward the hallway.

"No, wait!" I said, almost shouting. She couldn't get any farther or it would be over.

She turned around and stared at me. "What?"

"Uh, just be careful when you go in there," I said, my words coming out just as the plan was forming in my head. "Because of all the puking, I mean."

That stopped Sara cold. "Puking? You didn't say anything about puking."

"Oh yeah," I said, feeling the idea take shape. "Puking on

everything. You know, puking, fever—that's what the flu is all about. I just now got her cleaned up."

I could see Sara gag a little from the image. If there was one thing she couldn't stand, it was other people's bodily functions, and puking was pretty high on the list.

She turned back toward the front of the house and thrust the bag into my hands. It smelled like pot stickers, and my stomach suddenly started growling. Apparently the eggrolls from earlier were getting lonely down there. "Just tell her I came by, will you?" Sara pulled her coat tighter around her neck. "She is okay, right?"

"Oh yeah," I said, starting to relax. "There's really nothing for you to do." True, in more ways than one.

"It's freezing in here. Is the furnace out again?"

"Yeah," I said. "Phil needs to come over and deal with it."

"Want me to send Mark over tomorrow? He's pretty good with that sort of thing."

Sara and her boyfriend-fiancé-whatever, Mark, seemed to have worked out a pact to pretend our house was normal. He'd never spent any real time here, but he'd helped out a couple of times when things were broken, so he was more than aware of what he was dealing with. It made me wonder how she'd done it, because unless she was really good at hypnotism, he was a great actor. Or he was just stupid. "No," I said. "The space heaters are working okay. I've got one in my room."

"Be sure you keep it on so Mom doesn't get too cold."

I followed her to the front door, trying to ignore the irony of that last statement. "Yeah, I will. I'm sure she'll be okay in a couple of days. Well, I'll see you later." I could feel relief flooding my body as she put her hand on the knob.

Sara's eyes drifted around the big pile in the front hallway to the boxes I had sitting out on the floor by the recliner. "What's all that about?"

I turned to look at the boxes and bags lined up on the only visible floor space. "Oh, I, uh, . . ."

Sara marched over to them and peeked inside. She raised her eyes to meet mine with her mouth hanging open in disbelief. "Are you throwing her stuff out?" she hissed, her voice barely louder than a whisper. She picked up a couple of the old photos and junk mail I'd tossed into the bag. "Is this for the trash?"

"Just a few things. I thought I'd—"

"Does Mom know?" She pulled the photos out of the bag. "You're messing with Mom's photos? Man, she's going to kill you." Sara smoothed the edges of the photos that had gotten crumpled in the bag. She waved them at me. "None of this stuff belongs to you," she said, her voice getting a little bit louder. "You're sitting here while Mom is sick and can't defend herself, calmly tossing out her important things?"

After all I'd been through today I didn't need one of her lectures. I grabbed the top photo from her and held it out to her face. I was so sick and tired of everything, I was starting to lose my fear. "These aren't important," I said. "These are junk. You can't even tell what's in this photo—it's just a tangle of arms that are all out of focus."

Sara looked closer. "No, that picture was taken on the Fourth of July a couple of years ago. See, right there, that's the red, white, and blue shirt I always wear to the parade." She poked at it with a manicured finger. "You can't just get rid of Mom's stuff whenever you want."

I tossed the picture at her and it fell to the floor. "Fine, then," I said. "You take it. Otherwise it's going in the garbage with the rest of this useless crap."

Sara glared at me and slowly bent down to pick it up. "Useless crap? What the hell do you know about useless crap? After all Mom's done for you." She snatched the trash bag off the floor. "I'd better take this too so you don't throw away anything else important."

I could feel the anger bubbling in my chest again. I was tired of pretending nothing was wrong—that every family lived surrounded by head-high piles of garbage. That we didn't really want to have any friends over, and it didn't bother us when Mom made it seem like everything was our fault. "Come on Sara, look around this dump! It's full of nothing but moldy crap. We can't even live here properly because it's such a mess. You haven't slept in your room in years, because Mom filled it with piles of junk the minute you moved out. Same with Phil's room. Even Dad left this dump and never came back. I'm the one who has to live in it, and I'm sick of it!" I could feel angry tears welling up in my eyes. I hadn't cried all day, and now a stupid argument with Sara was threatening to make me all weepy.

"Stop being so selfish," she said. "It's not always about you, you know. It's not like I want to move back here or anything, so what do I care what she does with my room? And for your information, Dad didn't leave on his own—Mom kicked him out because he was constantly nagging her." Sara loved dropping little information bombs at the worst possible times. The fact that she was almost ten years older than me gave her lots of ammunition. She never let me forget that she was here long before me and that she never wanted to play the role of big sister.

"What are you talking about?" I asked cautiously. I never knew whether she was telling me the truth or not, because she often felt it was her duty to screw with me. "You know as well as I do Dad abandoned us to go live with what's-her-name. That's why Mom got stressed out about everything."

Sara waved that away with a flick of her wrist. "That's just what Mom says. I was almost your age when they got divorced, and it's not like I couldn't see or hear anything. Mom got tired of Dad not helping out. She said he made her life too difficult, so one day she just tossed him out on his ass. He didn't even meet Tiffany until way after that."

I stood staring at Sara, waiting for her to say more, but she seemed to have no idea this information completely contradicted everything I'd ever thought. She started filling the plastic bag with anything she could find.

"I can't believe you're taking advantage of Mom being sick by going through her stuff. Good thing I came by today, or God knows what you might have done." She looked up at me from where she was crouched on the ground gathering junk mail. "Mom told me she was worried about you. Always trying to keep her out of your room. What are you hiding in there? Hmm? Probably stealing stuff from Mom and squirreling it away. She always says that she can never find her valuables. You're probably taking them."

"Mom can't find anything because she lives like a pig!" I was practically shouting now, the image of late-night phone conversations between them feeding my frustration. "Are you blind? Look around! Stop defending her and look around. It's not healthy." I took a deep breath. "It's not normal."

"Well, then, maybe you should help more," she said.

"She's getting older and can't do everything for you. Now that she's working longer hours, she can't babysit you all day. When I was little, we helped out all the time, and this place was spotless. I'm sure that if you picked up after yourself every once in a while, it would get better."

"Now *you're* blaming me?" I didn't know why I was surprised—I'd heard it from Mom often enough. How I didn't help enough, and how if I were a better daughter, things would be okay. I shoved both arms at a teetering pile of clothes and bags until they toppled over onto the next pile.

"This is not my fault," I said slowly. It was the first time I'd ever said those words out loud, and I liked the way they felt. Sara might want to be just like Mom, but I was going to do everything I could to be different from the two of them. If I had to go and live on a tiny boat with nothing but a toothbrush and a change of underwear, I'd do it—I'd gladly leave all this behind just to have a normal life.

Sara stood up and took a few steps toward the hallway. "I'm going to have to wake Mom up and tell her what you've been up to. No matter how sick she is, she's going to want to know that she's being betrayed by her own daughter. Real nice, Luce."

As she began to work her way out of the room, I panicked, my resolve to stand up to them fading fast. Thank God it was too dark for her to see the growing pile of bags on the side of the house, but if she got down to the end of the hallway, she'd see Mom, for sure.

"No, don't!" I said. "Don't wake her up!" I flicked my hand and dumped a bunch of clothes on top of the other trash bags to cover them. Sara stopped walking and turned to me with her hand on her hip. There was just enough room in the pathway for her elbow to fit before it bumped the mounds of junk on either side. "I don't see that I have much choice," she said. She shook the bag at me. "Not after this."

I had to think fast. I should have known Sara would do this. "Look, I'm sorry," I said. I stared at the floor and tried to look as humble as possible. For once I was glad that I'd taken drama as an elective last year. I might not be able to deal with an audience of hundreds, but an audience of one I could handle. "I'm not tossing out Mom's stuff; I just wanted to make a little more space for her. It's getting so crowded around her chair, pretty soon she's going to be sleeping outside."

Sara looked over at Mom's chair and at the piles that were growing around it. "This is it?" she asked. She looked skeptical. "You didn't touch anything else?"

I could see her starting to change her mind. I had to keep talking. "No. Nothing. Only around the chair. I figured that when she was feeling better, it would be nice for her to be able to sleep without worrying that all of this was going to fall on her. You know . . . earthquakes and stuff."

Sara hesitated, and I could see that half of her still wanted to go tell on me. Nothing made her happier than to be the good daughter in Mom's eyes. She looked down at the bag in her hand. "Well, I'm still going to take this with me so you don't throw it away."

I followed her eyes as she looked around the rest of the room. Luckily, it was in such bad shape she couldn't tell if I'd done any work in here or not. I just had to keep her out of the dining room and the kitchen—not to mention the hallway. "Go ahead, if you want to," I said. Without knowing it, she could help me get at least one bag out of here.

"Oh, I want to." She turned to walk out the front door. As she passed me, she grabbed the bag of food I'd forgotten I was holding. "I'm taking this too. Get yourself something else to eat." Typical. If there was a way to fix things for me and Phil and leave her out of it, I would.

I followed her out the front door and down the walk toward the driveway. She thought I was just saying good-bye, but I was really making sure she was actually going. Sara had gotten a new car a couple of months ago, and even I was shocked to see what she'd done to it in such a short time.

The backseat was full of those cardboard file boxes I was sure she'd swiped from work. You couldn't see the floor because of the pile of discarded clothes that reached as high as the seat. The front seat could still hold a passenger, as long as that person was willing to wait for her to clear the empty CD cases, tissue boxes, clothes, shoes, and fast-food bags that covered both the seat and the floor.

Sara didn't seem to notice me staring. "I'll be back tomorrow to see how Mom's doing," she said as she climbed into the relatively clear driver's seat and grabbed at a water bottle that was rolling around by the brake pedal.

"Tomorrow?" I asked. I could feel the panic rising in my throat. I could never get it all done by tomorrow. Three days was bad enough. Tomorrow was impossible. "Aren't you working tomorrow?"

She glared at me. "I have a personal day coming, not that it's any of your business."

"What time tomorrow?" I could tell I said it too fast, even as the words burst out of my mouth.

Sara turned the key in the ignition. "That's for me to know," she said. "Stay away from her stuff."

"Don't worry about it," I said. I was sure I had enough worry growing in my stomach for both of us.

"Oh, but I do," she said.

I watched her back out of the driveway and take off down the street. It seemed like I exhaled for the first time since I'd seen her car in the driveway.

As I turned back toward the house, I realized that even when the mess was all cleaned up, it wasn't over. Mom was gone. But Sara was still very much around—and she was getting to be exactly like her.

chapter 14

7:00 p.m.

I twisted the dead bolt into place and leaned against the secure door. Between TJ, Mrs. Raj, and now Sara, this place hadn't seen so much action in years.

The smell of Chinese food still lingered in the hallway, and I realized how hungry I was. It was almost seven thirty, and all I'd had was a blueberry scone and a couple of eggrolls. Tomorrow for Sara probably meant somewhere around eleven at the earliest, which meant I had about sixteen hours to put things right in this house. My stomach would have to wait.

The house was quiet even though I could hear the stereo still playing faintly in the kitchen. Mom's TV sat almost buried in papers and clothes near her chair, but of course the remote was nowhere to be found. It could be buried just about anywhere, so I stood still and tried to think like Mom. If I needed the remote, where would I put it so it wouldn't get lost?

I couldn't see it anywhere around the chair or on the boxes that were next to it. Maybe underneath? If I wanted to be sure that I'd know where something was, I'd probably shove it underneath the one thing I knew wouldn't move.

I sat in the green chair and pushed it into a reclining position with my hands on the armrests, and then reached between the footrest and the chair. Touching something hard, I took a deep breath and stuck my hand as far under the chair as it would go. By flicking whatever it was to the side, I worked a corner of it out until I could grab it with one hand and drag it into the open.

Before I even pulled it out all the way, I realized it wasn't the remote. It was just a thick spiral notebook with a black cover. I could see from the bulge in the front there was something in it, but there wasn't anything written on the front. Her diary, maybe? I'd never seen Mom writing in anything, let alone a fairly large spiral notebook, but I had to admit that in the past few years we hadn't really paid that much attention to each other.

The book was pretty heavy, and it must be important if she kept it separate from all the other piles of junk in this place. If it was her diary, it would be wrong to open it. More wrong than leaving her dead in the hallway for the better part of a day? I shrugged my shoulders as I opened the black cardboard cover. It was all relative.

It wasn't a diary—not really. Carefully pasted onto the pages of notebook paper were magazine pictures of different houses. There was a picture of a wide, green lawn with a house perched way off in the distance and a family having a picnic on a postage-stamp-sized blanket. There were dining rooms with long tables where people could linger after a meal and talk about politics or sports. A bedroom with a white canopy bed

big enough for a mom and kids to curl up on a Sunday morning
and read the newspaper. Every now and then on the page would
be something written very carefully in her sprawling handwriting. She'd written "cabinets" next to the page with the rustic
kitchen and "knobs" next to a picture of some latches.

I flipped quickly through the rest of the book. Every picture showed a house in pristine photographic condition, the
people who lived there smiling at their good luck. There were
no clogged sinks, no green bins, and no giant stacks of newspapers.

The notebook wasn't her diary—it was more intimate than
that. They must have been pictures of the house *she* wanted to
have someday. Except that someday never showed up. I ran my
fingers over a picture of a wide porch with a swing that was
perfect for sitting with an iced tea on a hot summer night. She
must have been doing this for years—cutting out pictures of
what might have been. This book of possibilities completely
ignored the reality of what our lives had become. I knew how
she felt because I felt the same way when I thought about my
after. Hopeful—which was an emotion our house didn't see a
lot of.

I closed the cover and stared at it. How dare she have dreams
while making all of us live like this? She was the parent—she
could have done something about it. She was the one with
the power to make our lives like the people in the notebook,
but instead she buried us all under tons of filth and shame.

I crossed the room, the notebook heavy in my hands. It
made me angry and sad at the same time to picture her sitting
in her chair late at night carefully pasting other people's rooms
into her dream book. It was a small satisfaction when I tossed

the notebook unceremoniously into the trash bin. That's how much her dreams were worth in the face of my reality.

As I walked back toward the living room, my phone rang. "I've been trying to call you," I said as I flipped the phone open.

"What in the world did you do to Sara?" Phil asked without even bothering to say hello.

"Hey, Lucy," I imitated, ignoring his question. I was so angry at Mom right now that I needed to take it out on someone. "How are you doing? Was the rest of Christmas okay? Sorry I couldn't stay longer, but I have my own life now and can't be bothered with you people anymore."

"Ha, ha," he said flatly. "Point taken." I could hear him draw in a heavy breath, and the sound of some music in the background. "Okay, so how are you? And what in the hell did you do to Sara? I've spent the last half hour with her on the phone screaming in my ear about how ungrateful you are, and how I must have put you up to it."

I should have known Sara would call him. There was a green bin over near the wall, so I went to sit down on it. "I didn't do anything to her," I said. "She just came busting in here and started freaking out. You know how she always acts like she owns the place."

"So you're not doing what she said?" he asked. I could tell somebody was nearby because he was practically talking in code.

I looked around at the half-full garbage bags. "No." I hesitated for a second. "Maybe."

His voice cut out, and I could picture him switching the phone to his other ear. "What do you mean 'maybe'? Have you been . . . messing with her stuff? You know better than that."

I could hear another voice in the background. "Where are you, anyway?" I asked. "It sounds like you're at a party or something."

"I'm with Jen in the car," he said. "We're going up to Tahoe for a couple of days. And you didn't answer my question."

"I was just straightening up a few things around Mom's chair when Sara came in and did her usual favorite-daughter routine. It's no big deal."

"From the way she was talking, it sounded like you were dragging Dumpsters up to the front door and loading everything into them," he said. "Have you learned nothing? Leave it alone."

"I can't leave it alone." I said. "Not anymore."

"Less than two years, Lucy," he said quietly. "All you have to do is sit tight and wait until you graduate. Then you can do anything you want."

"I'm tired of waiting," I said, knowing everything had already been set in motion. As I looked around the room, I wished so badly that he would turn the car around and come help me. He was free to go to Tahoe for the weekend with his girlfriend, but I couldn't even go meet Josh at a party. I was tired of having it be *my* turn all the time. My turn to take care of Mom, my turn to worry about the house. When was it going to be *my* turn to get a life?

The resolve that I felt about being able to do this by myself was beginning to crack. I was sure that if I just told him the truth, he'd feel exactly like I did. If anyone in the world would understand how important this was, Phil would.

"How far away are you, exactly?" I asked.

"Placerville," he answered. "Why? Is something wrong? Sara said Mom was sick."

"Why haven't you ever brought Jen over to the house?" I'd met her a few times, and they'd come over to Bernie and Jack's house on Christmas, but she'd never been closer to the inside of our house than the driveway.

Phil's voice got lower. "Why are you asking that now?"

"It's important," I said. "I want to know why."

I could barely hear him over the car stereo as he answered. "You know why."

"Because of the mess? Because of the way we live?"

"Look, I don't want to get into this right now," Phil said. "I'll come over after I get back, and we can talk about it."

"I want to talk about it now," I said quietly. Why was I doing this all alone? Phil had just as much to lose—he should be here helping. I needed to tell someone. The pressure of keeping everything in was building, and I wouldn't be able to contain it much longer. Phil was the only solution. "Phil, there's something I have to tell you." I took a deep breath and just plunged in. "Mom . . ." I stopped, swallowed, and then tried again. "This morning I . . ."

My voice cracked as I surveyed the expanse of wall space that was smothered by stacks of newspapers and magazines that were as tall as I was. "I don't think I can handle this," I whispered.

Phil laughed a little. I think it was his attempt to sound soothing. "You can totally handle it," he said. "You're doing a great job. Just hold on a little longer, and you'll be living in the dorms at some swanky college somewhere. Have you thought about any applications yet?" He sounded a lot more confident as he tried to move the conversation into less touchy territory.

"Phil, I need your help. Right now. I need you to come home."

"Did . . . apply . . . summer . . ." His phone started to cut out.

"Phil?" I said loudly into the phone, but he was gone. I felt my entire body deflate. For the first time since he moved out, I felt like he was really and truly gone. He had successfully navigated Mom's house for his full sentence of eighteen years, and now that he was free, he didn't want to get dragged back into it. Not that I really blamed him. I'd probably do the same thing. Probably.

I sat staring at the phone until the light went out on the screen and the call ended. A year and a half. It wasn't that long if you were just trying to get through high school like a normal person. It would be a hell of a long time for someone called Garbage Girl who had no friends at all. The thought of Josh laughing at me along with everyone else was worst of all. I'd gotten so close to actually having what I wanted, but now all the good stuff was fading away.

I spent the next hour shoving trash into black plastic bags, but all of the optimism I'd felt earlier was gone. Who was I kidding? Sara was coming back in just a few short hours, and there was no way she was going to leave here without talking to Mom. The threat of puke had put her off this time, but it wasn't going to work forever. Everyone in town would know our secret by this time tomorrow.

My mind raced, picking up different scenarios for how my life was going to go. Maybe when Sara called the police, they wouldn't think the place was any big deal. Maybe nobody at school would even find out about the way we live and stare at me in the halls like the smell of rotting garbage billowed out behind me when I walked. Maybe Josh and Kaylie wouldn't care, and I'd get to have a best friend and a boyfriend at the same time. Maybe I was completely delusional.

I opened the dining room window and added several more bags to the growing pile. Mrs. Raj had her antennae up about the trash and would definitely come over to investigate. I wasn't sure if it was good or bad that she was the least of my problems at this point.

As I piled stuff into the big trash bags, I started to think about right after. After everyone knew Mom was gone, there would probably be a funeral. All the old ladies at church loved her for holding the rummage sale every year and organizing their senior meals. They would want to come. And the people at work would be there, Nadine for sure. Maybe even some of the families of "her people." But would they come once they'd found out the truth? Would the little old ladies and the friends from work be too horrified to show their faces at a memorial for Mom once she stopped being Joanna Tompkins and became that freaky garbage lady? I wondered if Dad would come, or if there were too many bad years between them for him to really care. I tried to picture the funeral with the casket and flowers, and me and Sara and Phil sitting in the front row all dressed up and looking sad.

The thing was, I didn't feel sad like I was supposed to. As I shoveled bags of clothes, work memos, and food wrappers into heavy-duty garbage bags, I felt a lot of things, but sad wasn't one of them. Angry, irritated, annoyed, lonely, and maybe even a little guilty. But not sad. Maybe after, I could be sad. But not now.

I might be able to survive senior year alone, but it would be so hard to watch Kaylie and Josh live their lives without me. I could just see myself in art class, sitting alone because nobody would want to come close enough to be my partner. Maybe I could graduate early, or do a home study until graduation. I could get a part-time job and live here with Phil until I could go away to college.

My phone was in my pocket, so I reached in to check the time. Seven fifteen. Depending on how late Sara stayed out to-night and how annoyed she actually was, I might have only twelve hours left. Sort of like Cinderella at the ball, only with garbage.

I made my way over to the front door and tried to imagine how the scenario would play out in the morning. I'd probably have to call 911 sometime before Sara actually showed up, and say that I found Mom lying in the hallway. Otherwise, it would look all wrong. Maybe the cops would put up that yellow tape, so Sara couldn't go sniffing around in here until everyone was gone.

As accomplished as I felt looking to the left of the front hallway, I felt completely deflated looking to the right. I must have spent at least three or four hours in there, and it was almost impossible to tell. Sure, I could see that there was more room around the old, soggy green chair, but nobody besides Sara was ever going to see the difference.

Straight ahead, the hallway narrowed into a two-and-a-half-foot space you could just squeeze through if you turned sideways, put your arms stiffly to your sides, and sucked in your breath. If you'd had a super burrito at El Gordito anytime in the past twenty-four hours, you didn't have a prayer of making it. I think that's one reason why Mom stayed so skinny all these years— navigating the house required a BMI of less than twenty.

The hallway took a sharp left at the end, and Mom was lying about four feet from the corner. Why couldn't she have died on her way out to get the paper? Or better yet, why not on the chair where she spent most of her time when she was home? Then it would be so much easier to get her out. But no. She had to die in the very back part of the very narrowest hallway, where it would be almost impossible for the paramedics to get her out on a gurney without lights flashing and hordes of neighbors straining to see what was going on behind the police barricades. Maybe they would just abandon the gurney idea altogether and just carry her body through to the front? Was there some sort of paramedic code that said that once a body was dead it had to be put in a body bag and strapped to a gurney, or did they have a little more leeway than that? Every dead body I'd ever seen on television had been sealed into black plastic and wheeled out on a bright yellow stretcher, but that didn't mean it was the rule.

I'd begun pacing in the free space in the front hallway. The constant movement actually helped me feel better—calmed my stomach and gave the butterflies something to do besides slam at my insides. I didn't know if it was all the coffee I'd had in the past twenty-four hours or just the fact that I could feel Sara getting closer by the minute, but I was starting to feel jumpy. If I could just figure out a way for the paramedics to get her out through the hallway, then maybe they'd be in and out fast enough for the house not to be such an issue. All they needed to do was check her over, make sure she was beyond CPR, get her out, and leave the condition of the house to me. If I could just make her more accessible, then her death would be normal. A woman dying under her own homemade avalanche made news. Somebody dying of lung problems or a heart attack happened every day.

I just had to make her more accessible. Accessible. The word bounced around in my head like a Ping-Pong ball. Accessible didn't have to mean they could get to her where she was— it just meant that they could get to her, period. Oh my God, what an idiot! I'd been working on this completely backward this whole time. Instead of bringing them through the front door to Mom, I needed to bring Mom to the front door!

I scooted sideways through the maze of trash until I reached the part of the hallway that took a sharp left toward her room. I stood at her feet and took a deep breath, staring at the tiny pink roses on the sheet that covered her. Each one looked like a painting that someone had spent hours and days to get just right— the shades of light and dark pink giving each flower a greater depth and dimension. Someone had to have bought it new at some point—probably not Mom, but someone. I'd bet they never would have guessed where the sheet with the cheerful pink roses was going to end up.

Reaching down to touch her, I swallowed hard and closed my eyes. The only way to get this done was to not think of this as Mom anymore. This wasn't the person who'd given birth to me and packed my lunches (well, for a few years, at least)—it was just a collection of bones and cells and duct-taped slippers that had to be temporarily relocated for the greater good. Greater good. I liked that. Made it sound almost biblical or something. I wasn't doing this for me so much as I was doing it for the greater good of Mom, Phil, and even Sara, although she didn't deserve it.

Blowing on my hands to warm them, I stood at Mom's feet and tried to find the best way to maneuver her through the narrow hallway. I was a lot taller than she was, but it would probably be too hard to stand her up, even though that would be the simplest way.

I squatted down and wrapped the end of the sheet a couple of times around her ankles so I'd have something to hold on to. Grabbing the sheet, I leaned back and pulled as hard as I could, grunting like a pro tennis player, until I lost my grip and tumbled backward on my butt, slamming into a stack of newspapers on the other wall and scrambling out of the way when they started to wobble.

There was no way she was that immovable. I gathered myself up and pulled again, but as I looked up toward her head, I could see that her shoulders were caught by the corner of one of the still-standing magazine piles. The pile shifted dangerously as I pulled one more time. Dropping her ankles, I picked my way over to the spot where she was stuck, held the top of the pile with my hand, and kicked at the bottom until the stack turned just enough to allow her shoulder to get by.

Taking my position down by her feet again, I pulled one more time, and she moved a few inches in my direction. After a few pulls, the sheet started to get dislodged from over her head, and I could see some of her white-rooted, wiry red hair sticking out of the top. I tried not to look as I pulled. It was much easier to concentrate on the grungy suede slippers. If I allowed myself to stop and think about what I was doing, I wouldn't be able to finish. I had to concentrate on the how and not think about the why, or it would seem too horrible and creepy.

When we reached the corner, I realized I couldn't pull her any farther. Because there were stacks of newspapers against all the walls, there was no easy way to get her around the turn and into the straight part of the hallway that led to the front door. If she would bend, it might work, but she'd been dead so long that there was very little give left in her body.

I should have stopped to try out a better strategy, but I felt that I just had to keep moving—I had to get this part over with as soon as possible. Cleaning the house didn't feel like such a big deal, but moving Mom meant that I had to make it look right. Cops notice when bodies are moved, and I was sure it was some sort of crime.

By picking my way around her body—and stepping on what I think was her left hand in the process—I made it to the other side up by her shoulders to try and ease her around the corner. If she had been alive she would have been really pissed at me right about now.

I could feel myself starting to get frustrated, but I breathed in slowly and tried to calm down. I was so close—only fifty more feet and it might be possible to actually be normal after all. Fifty lousy feet.

Looking at the one sharp corner that stood between me and success, the anger roiled in my stomach, and I so badly wanted to scream and kick the stacks that surrounded us. The turn was so sharp and the path was so narrow—there was no way to get her around the corner. Relocating her was such a good idea and it made too much sense to *not* work.

Like everything else in this whole stupid day, I had failed again. Just like Mom and Sara always said—I couldn't do anything right. Even dead, Mom seemed to be laughing at me, lying there refusing to make it easy once again.

It would serve everybody right if I walked out of the house at that moment—straight down the driveway—and left all this crap behind me. Just turned my back on all of it and kept on going. Not that I had anywhere *to* go, but as long as it wasn't here, it really didn't matter. I imagined how it would feel to walk down the street with nothing in my hands and not worry about this house. I bet it would feel amazing. Free. There was nothing stopping me from doing it. It's not like there was a lock on the door, or someone telling me I couldn't go. Anytime I wanted to, I could just head out the door and let someone else deal with all this mess.

Except I knew that I wouldn't. It was up to me to deal with this, just like it had been up to me to take care of us these last few years, making sure Mom ate a decent meal once in a while and had enough clean clothes for work. It was up to me to make sure the plumbing still worked and we weren't reduced to peeing in buckets again. Up to me to make sure that nobody ever found out how bad Mom was getting. It was still up to me.

My body felt disconnected from my brain as I tucked in the sheet once again. Mom's arms were flung sideways near her head, but I couldn't bring myself to grab her hands, so I lifted her under the arms and pulled her back down the hallway just a little bit, so her feet weren't all jammed up in the corner and she wasn't visible from the front door. I sat in the hallway a few inches from her head and tucked my knees up under my chin.

I told myself that I was just taking a break—I wasn't giving up—but I wasn't sure I believed me.

I felt empty and used up. As I sat, gazing at the floor, I noticed her left hand was brushed up against my leg, almost like she was reaching out to touch me. It was such an unusual gesture for her to make that it startled me. I looked at her unpainted fingernails with the ridges that had gotten deeper the past few years and wondered when she'd touched me for the last time. We'd never been a very "touchy" family, but I couldn't remember holding her hand or even feeling her fingers brush against mine as we passed something to each other recently.

Looking at the hand that had made such an unbelievable mess of things, I realized it was also the hand that had carefully pasted pictures of what she wanted her life to be like into a notebook—the hand that had stroked the feet of a lonely, dying woman.

I reached out and curled my hand around her still, icy fingers. I held it there for a long time as I sat with my knees to my chest, wishing that just for a minute she could squeeze it back and tell me everything would be okay.

chapter 15

8:00 p.m.

It was pointless to keep going but impossible to stop. I wandered aimlessly around the house, trying to decide what to do next, finally sitting down on the arm of Mom's chair to psych myself up for the long night ahead.

Something was sticking up from the back corner of the cushion. The remote, maybe? I leaned over and pulled out a pair of scissors. Special scissors with black handles. Cautiously, I stuck my hand farther down into that corner and felt something hard and narrow. Another pair of scissors, but these had blue handles.

I finally pulled up three pairs of scissors scattered around the edges where the cushion met the chair. It was just like Mom. She was the one who lost the scissors down here, and when she couldn't find them, she went out and bought another pair. After she blamed me for losing them, that is. I took the cushion off to see what else had been right under her butt the whole time.

There were a few coins of different sizes and some old popcorn kernels sharing space with over a dozen envelopes that were piled toward the front of the seat. The coins and scissors I could understand, but how would sealed envelopes just happen to fall underneath the front of the cushion? And in a nice, neat stack?

I picked one up and looked at the return address. It was from a bank and it was pretty thick. Maybe she had a secret bank account she didn't want us to know about. Mom always said we didn't have enough money for things that I wanted, but I never believed her because she had Dad's child support plus what she made at the hospital. I had to pay for my own cell phone, and I'd missed the tenth-grade trip to Disneyland last year because we supposedly couldn't afford it. The main reason I didn't get my license wasn't because I had no car, but because Mom said the extra insurance would be too expensive. I always suspected that saying we couldn't afford it was an easy way for her to get out of something she didn't want me to do. It would be just like her to be literally sitting on a fortune.

Sliding one finger under the envelope flap, I allowed myself a spark of excitement. There might be enough in here to really make a difference. I could get the car fixed and get my license so I wouldn't have to rely on other people to get everywhere. Maybe I'd buy a new car instead—one that didn't remind me of Mom every time I sat in the driver's seat. One that would take me as far as I wanted to go.

I ripped the envelope all the way open and took out the papers that were inside. Ever since I started earning my own money, I'd been getting bank statements, so I knew one when I saw one. And this wasn't one. It was from a credit card company. There were pages and pages of charges, and on the first page in big black letters was one of the largest numbers I'd seen in real life. I looked up at the date in the corner of the page. This statement was from six months ago, but even then Mom owed $48,562 to this credit card. With all of the Christmas stuff she'd bought last month, I was sure the total was now a lot higher. I frantically pawed through the envelopes from all the other banks. The next bill I opened was newer and had another huge number in the corner. The next showed a balance of only $9,867. In the space of just a few seconds, $9,867 had started to feel like "only."

The handle of her purse was sticking up beside the recliner. Mom always kept it in the same spot so it wouldn't get swallowed up in the tide of garbage. The panic was rising as I reached into it and pulled out her wallet. It was the same worn brown leather wallet she'd carried since I could remember, bulging at the sides, with scraps of paper receipts sticking out the top. Carefully, I opened the snap and looked inside. The slots were filled with credit cards—some were grocery cards or insurance cards, and one was a library card, but most of them were credit cards. As I pulled them out, I examined the expiration dates— it would be just like Mom to carry around a lifetime's worth of expired credit cards—but all of these were current.

There were two cards with airplanes on the front, one with a panda bear, a Macy's, a Target, and one from a store I'd never even heard of. When her wallet was empty, there were twelve credit cards sitting in front of me. All of a sudden, I felt like I couldn't breathe.

The mountains of stuff seemed to vibrate as I shifted my glance from one pile to the next. I thought about the ice-skating lessons I wasn't allowed to take because they were too expensive, and the week at the lake that turned into three days at a

Motel 6 in Modesto because it was a lot cheaper. The scholar-
ships and grants I was chasing because there wasn't enough
money to go to a good university without a lot of help. And
this is where it had all ended up. Not in trips to the beach, or a
remodeled kitchen. It had ended in late-night home-shopping
bargains on stuff we'd never use and gifts for people she would
never give. That pile of plastic had fueled this pile of worthless
garbage. Instead of seeing just piles of clothes and junk, I realized for the first time how much money must have been involved
in amassing this much stuff. How much had she spent on things,
only to have them sit in a pile for months and years? Whenever
I bought a new book, Mom would remind me that there was a
library in town, and libraries were free. Thank God I had Dad's
money, because Mom's was only for stuff that was important to
her. Apparently, that included useless countertop mixers, but did
not include me.

My stomach was in knots as I thought of having to pay it
all back. What if being dead meant that you weren't off the
hook? It would take years—decades, probably—to pay back all
the money she owed. There was no way I could afford to go to
a good school now. If I was lucky, I might have time for junior
college between jobs, if I had to help pay all that money back.
Josh and Kaylie would go off to freshman year at UC Berkeley
or Stanford and I'd be . . . where exactly? Where would I be?

I grabbed each stack of credit card bills and flung them
across the room, as if getting rid of the evidence would make
the problem go away. My jaw clenched as I reached for an arm-
load of newspapers and threw them into the middle of the
room, only to have them settle on the piles like a small dusting
of snow on a glacier. A scream rose from the back of my throat

as I lunged toward a stack of books and newspapers next to her chair and brought them crashing down with a vibration so strong the walls shook. I grabbed anything I could reach, enjoying the thud as whatever it was hit the wall and bounced back into the room. The sharp sound of the vase breaking against the brick fireplace was still ringing in my ears when I noticed a small trickle of blood from a tiny gash in the side of my hand. Staring at the smear of red that ran from the cut, I wiped it with my other hand until it started to sting. The pain had a weird calming effect and I doubled over, breathing heavily like I'd been sprinting.

I couldn't spend another second in that house. I had to get out if I was going to keep hold of my sanity and salvage anything. Stacks of books and newspapers fell to the floor as I raced down the pathways, focusing only on reaching the front door so I could breathe again.

The cold air hit me as I yanked the open door, and I drank it in as I moved toward the darkness. My breath was making little puffs of fog but I didn't feel cold. Here, I was free from the pathways and the stale decay of the house. Out here, there was no ceiling to trap the mess, only the stars that promised the vastness of space with nothing between me and them but cold, clean air.

I reached the corner and stood under the streetlight watching the traffic signals change from green to yellow to red and back again like they were part of a universal rhythm. I had no plan, only vague thoughts that passed through my head like vapor, only to disappear as quickly as they had formed.

Without realizing I was even moving, I found myself standing in front of Kaylie's house. I stared at the front door and tried to decide if knocking was what I really wanted to do. The minivan was in the driveway, and I could see a light on in her window upstairs.

"Lucy!" she squealed when she answered the door. "Why didn't you call? We totally would have come picked you up."

"It's okay," I said, amazed that my lips were moving in a coherent manner. "I needed the walk."

"Is your mom better?"

"About the same," I whispered. I felt like I was watching everything happen from very far away. It was safer than being inside my body and feeling empty.

"Well, I'm glad you changed your mind," she said. "I was just getting ready to go—Vanessa's sister is picking me up on the way." She turned her head and looked at me more closely. "You okay? You look like hell."

I ran my hand over my hair and could feel it sticking up in more than a few places. "Oh, yeah," I said. "I just didn't have a chance to—"

"Not to worry. You've come to the right place." I climbed the stairs to her room a few steps behind her. "I got this killer new straightener that will work magic on your hair. That and a few swipes of Plum Sable eye shadow should have you back on track."

We passed the bathroom, and I realized that what I really wanted was to stand still somewhere and let stinging droplets of hot water wash this entire day down the drain. "Actually, Kaylie, could I, uh, take a shower maybe?"

"Okay," she said, apparently not thinking it was a weird request. "But make it quick."

My brain whirred on empty as I stood under the pounding water, feeling it flow over my shoulders and down my back. For the first few minutes I just stood there soaking, inhaling the steam and the heat, breathing it deep into my lungs. I grabbed the washcloth Kaylie had given me, lathered with sharp, clean-smelling citrus soap, and scrubbed until my skin was raw. Shampoo was dripping down my face when the door to the bathroom opened.

"Lucy?" Kaylie said as she tiptoed in. I had tucked Teddy B. into my jacket, which was folded on the floor, and I prayed she wouldn't see him. I'd forgotten I even had him on me, but now that he was here, it seemed important that he stay secret. "I brought you those jeans that are too long for me and that cute black-and-white-striped shirt that made me think of you when I bought it. No offense, but if we're going to the party, you need something else to wear."

I rinsed and stuck my head out of the curtain. "Thanks," I said. All I wanted was to curl up in a ball in the corner of the room and sleep for about a hundred years.

"If you're going to get Josh Lee, you have to look hot. Hurry up so I can do your hair and stuff before we go."

I wished I had left my toothbrush over here, as I rinsed my mouth with toothpaste. My clothes were in a heap on the floor, so I rolled them into a tight ball and stuck them behind the door. They were just one more reminder of what I'd left behind, and it would be fine with me if I never saw them again. Holding my jacket to my nose, I sniffed to see if the mold and the garbage and the mess had gotten deep into the fibers. It seemed okay, but just to be sure, I sprayed it lightly with the perfume Kaylie had on the counter. I tucked Teddy B. into my jacket and zipped it up over him. I didn't know why, but I felt calmer with him pressing into my side.

Kaylie looked me over as I came into her room. "What's with the jacket? Are you still cold?"

I zipped the jacket up higher. "A little."

"Sometimes you have to sacrifice comfort for fashion."

"I'll take it off when we get there," I lied. Actually going somewhere, especially somewhere that Josh was going to be, seemed impossible, but I felt like I was being carried downstream in a strong current that had nothing to do with me.

"Okay, sit down here."

I sat numbly on her bed while she hovered around with a little dash of this and a little dab of that. The blow-dryer felt nice on my neck, and I let her do what she wanted while I sat and thought about absolutely nothing. I came back to the present as she clipped the metal plates on my hair until they sizzled.

"Ow!" I jerked away from the iron.

"Ooh, sorry!" she said. She rubbed my ear. "I do that all the time." She took a step back and admired her work. "You look awesome. Between the haircut and the straightener, it's just a little badass. Close your eyes."

She sprayed a nice-smelling mist over my head. "That ought to last the rest of the night."

I peeked around her until I could see myself in her mirror. It didn't look that bad. My hair stuck out like it did before I washed it, only now it looked as if it were on purpose. My eyelids wore a shade of purple so dark they looked vaguely bruised.

"Josh is going to freak out," she said. "You should wear makeup all the time."

I shrugged and made a face. I could pile the entire drawerful of stuff on my face and it wouldn't make any difference. Not after tomorrow, anyway.

"Seriously," she said as she unplugged the straightener. "I think he's totally into you, and this is going to prove it." Kaylie rubbed her hands together. "I promised Vanessa I'd be ready at nine, so we should go downstairs. This is going to be great. Maybe if you hook up with Josh, he'll ask you to the Spring Formal. You're so lucky."

I tried to think that far ahead, but my thoughts ran into a deep black hole. Nothing existed beyond tomorrow when Sara came home and found out what had happened. All of a sudden I knew I couldn't go through with it. There was no way I could go and be with people and act normal. Not with my entire life unraveling by the minute.

"You go ahead," I said, my voice shaky. "I can't. I'm just going to . . . I'm just going to go home."

Kaylie looked concerned. "What's the matter? Are you sick?"

"I just . . . I . . ." I slid to the floor and put my hands over my face. It felt like a wave filled with everything wrong with my life was crashing over me—Mom lying under the sheet, mountains of garbage that I could never fix even if I had months instead of hours, piles of bills that threatened everything we had left, and images of our neighbors shaking their heads as they looked through our open doors at the truth we'd been so careful to hide all these years. I felt myself gasp as the tears started to roll down my cheeks, and I brought my knees up to my chest. I couldn't believe I was actually sitting on Kaylie's rug bawling like a baby, but there was nothing I could do to stop it.

Kaylie knelt next to me. I could feel her arm around my shoulder and smell her perfume, but I didn't dare take my hands away from my face. What if I broke down and told her the truth? "Lucy," she said softly. "Hey, Luce, what's going on? Come on, whatever it is, we can fix it." One hand patted my shoulder as she held me closer.

"There's nothing you can do," I whispered, my voice raggedy with crying. "There's nothing anybody can do. It's over."

"Listen, listen," she said, trying to pry my hands from my eyes. "I'm your best friend, right? Right?"

I nodded, but the thought brought a fresh batch of tears coursing down my face. For the next few hours she was, but then what?

"Then you've got to tell me what's wrong," she said. "I can't help you if you won't tell me."

"I can't," I said. I took a couple of deep breaths and tried to get a grip. The back of my hand was streaked with purple and black smudges where I'd wiped my eyes. "It's just . . . I can't." She'd understand soon enough when the news broke. It's not like she could help me, anyway, even if I told her everything. I should just let her think I'd had a fight with Mom or had a bad case of PMS. She'd never guess what was really wrong with my life. "I'm okay," I said, wiping the makeup from under my eyes.

Kaylie knelt next to me and grabbed my hand. "You're obviously *not* okay," she insisted. "Is it your mom?" I shook my head. "Is it Josh?"

"No. Yes. I don't know," I said. "It's just everything." Bracing myself against the wall, I pulled myself up. "I'm sorry.

That was so stupid. Really, I'm fine." If Kaylie didn't think I was a loser before, I was sure she did now.

"You're sitting here looking like the world is ending, and you expect me to believe you're fine? Lucy, you have to be honest with me. I'm your best friend—you at least owe me that."

And for a sliver of a second I thought about it. Thought about telling her everything—about Mom, the house, the bills— but as much as I wished she'd stay concerned and caring, I was just as sure that she wouldn't. Kaylie was the nicest friend I'd ever had, but she wasn't a superhero.

"Do you want to stay home?" she asked. "Because I can just call Vanessa—"

I took a deep breath. "No. No, let's go." And I meant it. No matter what I was doing, nothing was going to happen at the house until morning. The next twelve hours were going to be the last normal ones in my life, and I didn't want to waste them surrounded by garbage at my house or sitting in a heap on her floor. This would be the last chance I ever had to be just regular old Lucy, and I might as well go out and make the most of it. I sniffed, and wiped the last traces of moisture from my face. "I must be a wreck," I said, laughing a little.

Kaylie grinned, but her eyes still looked serious. "You did sort of ruin my work," she said. "Sit down and I'll fix it for you, if you're sure."

I nodded quickly, and she got out some wipes and the makeup and started repairing the damage I'd caused.

Kaylie's mom knocked at the same time she stuck her head in the doorway. "Oh, hi, Lucy," she said, giving me a smile. "I didn't hear you come in." She turned to Kaylie. "Who's driving tonight?"

"Vanessa's sister. She's home from college for vacation. I was thinking one o'clock—it's break, after all."

"Twelve thirty," her mom said. "But no later. And make sure she isn't drinking. You can always call me if you get stuck." It always blew me away that Kaylie and her mom could talk about those kinds of things. Mom would freak if I went to a party, forget about one where she thought there might be drinking.

"Are you spending the night, Lucy?" her mom asked me. She never asked why I spent so much time over here—she seemed to know she wouldn't like the answer.

"Yes," Kaylie said quickly.

"Actually, I have to go home tonight," I said. I had to get home before Sara to make sure everything looked right before I ended it all with a simple phone call.

"Well, you're always welcome here. You know that. I'll see *you* at twelve thirty." She put her arm around Kaylie and kissed her on the cheek—a gesture that neither of them gave a second thought but made my heart ache.

"You really okay?" Kaylie asked, reaching for her purse. " 'Cause you can tell me anything."

I shrugged, not trusting my voice, and stared off into the distance, trying to maintain some control. She had no idea what "anything" might mean.

"Listen," she said, turning off her bedroom light. "The stars are aligning. I can feel it. This is going to be your night. It's going to be great." The more she spoke, the more excited Kaylie seemed to get. It was hard not to catch a little bit of her enthusiasm.

"If you say so," I managed.

"Well, I do say so." She looked me up and down and brushed some stray hairs away from my face. It was such a caring gesture that it almost made me start crying again.

"Thanks," I said quietly. At least for tonight I had a real best friend. I stood a little straighter, trying to be one of those people who took chances. "Okay, let's go." I didn't look back as we walked out of the house and into the last normal night of my life.

chapter 16

9:00 p.m.

Vanessa's sister pulled up just as we got outside. She slid the back door open and then grabbed her phone to answer a quick text.

"Hey, Lucy," Vanessa said from the front seat as we climbed into the minivan. "I didn't think you were coming."

In the split second between when she spoke and when I answered, a million thoughts ran through my brain. Did she *wish* I wasn't coming? Had she and Kaylie been talking about me behind my back about tonight? Vanessa and I were like friends once-removed. We wouldn't have had any connection at all except for Kaylie, and I always felt like she was letting me know that she had been there first.

"Yeah," I said. "I got done early so I decided to come along."

Kaylie smacked me on the shoulder. "She got done early and couldn't stand the thought of Josh Lee being there all by himself." She sat back hard as the van lurched into the street.

"Are you having a thing with Josh Lee?" Vanessa asked in a tone that said she didn't believe it.

"No," I said. "Kaylie's just hallucinating." I could feel my cheeks getting warm at the thought of seeing him. Focusing on Josh made my nerves calm down a little. I had to put Mom and the house behind me if I was going to go through with this. This was my only shot, and I had to take it because there probably wouldn't be another one.

"Not even," she said. "You should have seen them at the movies last night."

God, was that really only last night? It seemed like weeks ago.

"That's funny. I thought he was back together with Cara," Vanessa said. I was pretty sure she was lying, but the thought made my stomach turn. Still, it wouldn't be that surprising—they were bound to get back together at some point. Vanessa grinned at me as she sat back in her seat and pulled a cigarette out of her purse. She'd taken a few drags when Kaylie smelled it and popped the back window open.

"Nessa!" she yelled. "My mom will have a heart attack if she smells smoke on me!"

"All right, all right," Vanessa said, leaning forward to toss the cigarette out the front window. "Calm down. You act like you've never seen anyone smoking before."

Kaylie waved her hands around the interior of the van, trying to coax the smoke outside. "I've never seen you smoking before. What were you thinking? You know your mom would kill you for stinking up her van."

Vanessa reached into her purse and pulled out a pack of Camel 100's. "She wouldn't care. Besides, these things totally help you lose weight," she said. "They're kind of expensive, but cheaper than diet pills as long as you buy them by the carton."

"Just stay away from me with those," Kaylie said. "I don't need to get grounded."

Vanessa's sister parked behind a long line of cars on the normally quiet street. Even inside the van we could hear music coming from a house halfway up the block. I felt a strange thrill run through me at the thought of Josh being so close. "I'm not getting the rest of my winter break wrecked because you need to be skinnier," Kaylie said.

"Whatever," Vanessa said and opened the door. "There's Tricia! Hey, I'll meet you guys up there." She hopped out of the van as delicately as someone who is wearing a super-short miniskirt can. "Trish! Wait up!"

I watched Vanessa walk up the dimly lit street, her multi-hued blond hair waving behind her like a shimmering stream and the three-inch heels she was wearing not slowing her stride a bit. I envied Vanessa not because most of her butt was hanging out of her skirt—that just made me feel colder—but because she truly never cared what other people thought of her. She'd say something mean about someone, something that most everyone had probably been thinking, anyway, but the difference was she'd say it to their face. That kind of behavior didn't make people hate her like you'd think it would. Instead, it made most people hope that they weren't the one she was talking about. She had always left me pretty much alone. So far.

Kaylie wriggled out of the backseat and jumped to the ground. "Let's do it."

I'd left the house so quickly I didn't have anything with me, and it made me feel kind of naked. I stuck my hands in my jacket pockets to warm them. Teddy B.'s leg was near the left pocket under my jacket, and I gave it a little squeeze for luck or courage or something.

I tried to be cool as we walked into the party. A few people I didn't recognize weren't so much dancing as swaying in the middle of the living room floor. One girl dressed in a pink sweater was draped over the shoulders of a short guy in saggy jeans. She looked like she was sleeping.

"Most people are probably out back," Kaylie said, and, grabbing my hand, pulled me toward the sliding glass doors at one end of the room.

It was so cold outside that there were puffs of steam hovering just over everyone's heads as they exhaled. At the back of the patio on a small raised deck, Josh stood with a guitar slung low on his hips and one hand on the microphone. He was wearing a thin T-shirt and jeans, in contrast to everyone else who was bundled in down jackets and scarves. The muscles in his arms were marked by ropy veins that pulsed every time he played a chord on the guitar. Even from back here I could see the sweat dripping down the side of his temples, and the front of his hair was plastered to his forehead. There was a group of people gathered around the makeshift stage, with a bunch of girls lining the front. The waves of desire between the crowd and the band were almost physical as Josh began to sing, his eyes closed with the effort. All of a sudden I wished I hadn't come. Josh could have any girl here—why did I think he'd want me? That he had his arm around me just a few hours ago seemed suddenly impossible.

I felt like I did the one and only time we'd spoken at school earlier this year—stupid and delusional. I'd been standing by my locker shifting books out of my backpack when I saw him a

few feet away talking to Steve Romero. I heard Steve slam his
locker and walk away, which is why I was totally startled to see
Josh still standing there as I turned to go to class.

"Hey," he said, smiling at me, either not noticing or ignoring the fact that I jumped a mile. "We have physics together,
don't we?"

"Mmm hmm." I nodded. I didn't trust myself to say actual
words.

"You're Lucy, right?" he said, not waiting for an answer.
"I'm Josh. Josh Lee."

"I kn—" I realized almost too late that "I know" would be
kind of obvious. "Right," I finally said, managing a tight smile.
"Yeah, I'm Lucy. Tompkins."

He turned to go and I stood there hyperventilating like an
idiot, not believing we had an almost-conversation. After a few
steps, he turned back to look at me. "Come on," he said. "We'd
better hurry if we're going to make it before the bell."

I took a few quick steps to catch up to him. "Right," I said.
"Physics." Our strides matched as we walked down the hall, me
racking my brain trying to come up with something interesting
to say. Luckily, Josh didn't seem to have the same problem.

"God, Ms. Lucas is killing me this year," he said. "I thought
chemistry was bad, but sometimes it's like she's speaking another
language."

"It's not so hard," I said. Art was my favorite subject, but I
always did pretty well in science too. I watched our feet as they
stretched over the worn linoleum floor, not daring to look up into
his face. "She usually explains things pretty well. Plus, physics is
kind of fun if you look at it the right way."

"Are you kidding me?" Josh asked. "Fun? No wonder

you're always getting As. We should study together sometime, just so I don't screw up my GPA. Then you can show me how physics is fun."

I glanced up to see if he was kidding, but he was looking at me seriously out of the corner of his eye. "Um, we could do that," I said. "That would be cool." I couldn't believe that Josh Lee was actually walking through the hall asking me to help him with physics. Maybe we could go to the café and study, our heads bent over one of the tiny round tables as we ordered coffee after coffee to keep us working until late at night.

Josh's smile widened. "Maybe—"

"There you are!" Cara squealed, jumping on his back and draping her arms over his shoulders. "I've been looking all over for you." She buried her face in his neck, and I just stared, wishing so badly I had permission to do the same thing.

He reached up and grabbed her by the arms. "Hey, Cara," he said, laughing a little. "We were just heading to class."

Cara slid off his back. "We?" she asked.

"Yeah." He nodded in my direction. "You know Lucy?"

She glanced at me for a second longer than necessary and said, "Um, not really." Cara turned her full attention to Josh. "Listen, I need to talk to you about Friday night." She pulled him over to the lockers and leaned in so they could talk quietly, leaving me standing alone in the stream of people heading to class. I watched for a second as they surrounded themselves with the privacy that only long-time couples seem to have—studying each other, oblivious to everyone else around them.

"Well," I said quietly and sighed. "Guess I'll see you in class." I walked slowly toward the science wing, feeling like an idiot but also grateful that I hadn't made a complete ass of myself. Like Josh would ever choose me over Cara. Or over anyone.

Now here I was doing the same thing again—having crazy fantasies about Josh when he was just being polite. Kaylie stood on her tiptoes surveying the crowd. "I think I see Steve over to the right."

"I'm freezing," I said. "I'm going back inside." I wanted to get out of there before Josh knew I'd come. I couldn't compete with all of the normal girls in school—there was no use even trying.

"What's inside?" Kaylie asked. "All the good stuff is out here." She looked at me and then back to the band. "What you need is some beer. Wait here, I'll be right back."

With the crowd around the keg as huge as it was, I figured she'd be gone for ages, but she was back in a minute or two.

"Here," she said, handing me a blue plastic cup. "Careful, it's a little drippy."

"How did you do that so fast?"

"I have my ways," she said. She looked over my shoulder to see if Steve was still there. I wished I could be more like her and look straight at what I wanted. And navigate a keg in under two minutes. "Drink it quick. It'll relax you."

I took a tentative sip of the beer. It tasted like vomit. I tried hard not to wrinkle my nose in disgust.

"Is it bad?" Kaylie asked. I handed her the beer and she took a small sip. "Just like them to get a keg full of crap beer." She handed it back to me. "Doesn't matter, though, it'll do the trick."

Vanessa and Tricia came over with their own matching blue plastic cups. The beer was cold and my hand was getting numb. They should give you those cardboard sleeves like they do at Sienna when the coffee is too hot for the cup.

"Cheers!" Vanessa said, and raised her cup in the air before taking a giant swig. She didn't even make a face when she was done.

"Are we checking out anyone in particular?" Tricia asked. Her skirt was almost as short as Vanessa's, but at least she had the decency to shiver and cross her arms in front of her as she tried to ward off the cold wind that cut through the yard.

Vanessa laughed. "Apparently Miss Lucy here has a thing going with Josh Lee."

Tricia raised her eyebrows. "I knew that he'd broken up with Cara—were you his thing on the side?"

"No way!" Kaylie answered for me. "Get real. Lucy doesn't have to go for sloppy seconds. Josh asked her to come to the party. He's totally into her."

"If he's so into her, then why has he been flirting with Justine all night?" Tricia asked. She tossed her head in the direction of the stage.

I felt a heavy weight settle in my stomach as I looked back toward the rear of the yard. Sure enough, Justine had planted herself right in front of where Josh was singing.

"He's not flirting with Justine," Kaylie said. "Everyone knows she's been throwing herself at him for months."

"I have eyes," Tricia said. "And I know what I saw." She looked at me. "You don't seriously think you'd be going out with him? He's totally going to get back together with Cara— they're just cooling off until after winter break. They're meant for each other."

Each word was like a hammer blow of reality. Kaylie might

want to think Josh liked me, but as annoying as Tricia was, she was probably right. I glanced back to the stage where Josh was looking intently at someone as he finished the song. He was looking right at Justine Hildebrandt.

The music stopped, but I couldn't bear to have Josh see me now, chasing him like all the other girls. What would he think if he saw me standing here? I couldn't stand to see him put his arm around Justine, to know that she was feeling the warmth of his body next to hers, inhaling his scent. The last normal night of my life was probably going to end like every other one had—with me cold and alone.

Kaylie was still arguing with Tricia, so I inched backward until I was standing next to a tall palm tree in a big wooden planter. I tried taking another drink to see if getting buzzed would make me feel any better, but the beer was so disgusting I could barely manage a tiny swallow. There was no way I was going to be able to choke down enough to make it worth it— while nobody was looking I tipped my cup into the planter and dumped out half the beer.

As I raised the cup back to my lips so it would look like I'd been drinking the whole time, I felt warm breath on the back of my neck.

"I wouldn't drink that swill, either," he said with a laugh.

My heart raced and I didn't know whether to be happy or horrified, because I'd recognize Josh Lee's voice anywhere.

chapter 17

9:30 p.m.

"Well, well," Vanessa said. "Look who's here."

I bit the edge of my plastic cup and stared down at my shoes, not daring to look behind me. I knew that if I turned around and saw Josh holding hands with Justine, I'd probably run out of there without another word. So much for acting normal.

"I'm going to get something to drink," Josh said, slightly out of breath. "Can I get anybody anything?"

He was standing so close to me I could feel the heat radiating off his body. He smelled clean and solid as he spoke over my shoulder. One quick glance told me that, at least for the moment, he was alone. I'd never believed the whole "weak in the knees" theory, but right now I wasn't sure I was going to be able to stay upright.

I looked up in time to see Vanessa cut her eyes at me. She tossed her long blond hair behind her shoulder and raised her eyebrows. I didn't know what she was up to, but it didn't feel good. "I'd love another beer," she said. She rolled her tongue over her lips and giggled as he took her cup.

As far as I knew, she didn't even like Josh, so the only reason for the theatrics was to get him to notice her. And in that skirt and with those heels, if he didn't notice her, he was blind.

"What about you, Luce?" Josh asked. "You look like you could use another beer." I swear he winked at me when he said it.

I pretended to take another sip from my cup. "No, thanks. I'm fine." If I got more beer, the potted plants on the patio would probably wither up and die before the night was over.

"Well, at least help me carry these." Josh tucked my arm into his and spun me around.

I was so surprised I started sputtering. "Wait . . ."

Kaylie grinned as I looked over my shoulder at her. "Go on, Lucy—Josh looks like he needs help."

Josh guided me effortlessly through the crowd and in through the patio doors to the kitchen. His cheeks were bright red from playing and his hair was damp with sweat. "Here we are," he said, and set the cups down on the counter.

"But the keg's out there," I said.

"I've got something better in here," Josh said, and pulled the refrigerator door open. "Rinse those out, will you?" His voice was muffled as he dug through the crammed fridge.

I had no idea what he was doing, but I turned on the tap and rinsed our cups under hot water. The beer in the keg was nasty, and I wasn't up for drinking any more, but I could always find somewhere to dump it out.

Bottles clanked as Josh emerged from the depths of the

fridge. "Here we go. I had to stash them way back there so nobody would drink them."

"Must be special," I said. "I didn't think to bring my own." I was nervous, so I was monitoring everything that came out of my mouth. It was like there were two people in my body—one who was actually speaking to Josh and one who was hanging back and making sure that the one doing the talking didn't sound completely stupid.

"Hand me your cup." Josh took one bottle and put the end of his shirt over the cap as he twisted it off with a sound like air escaping from a tire. He poured some into my cup and handed it back to me. For the shortest of seconds, our fingers brushed and my whole arm began to tingle.

The beer in my cup had a big brown head of foam on it. I sniffed it like I knew how good beer was supposed to smell.

"Try it," Josh said. His brown eyes crinkled up in a nice way as he grinned at me. "It's good stuff. Imported."

I tipped the cup and took a sip. It was good—sweet and spicy.

"Root beer," Josh leaned in and whispered. He touched his forehead to mine and laughed quietly. "It didn't look like you were enjoying the keg, so I thought you might want something else. I'm driving tonight, so I brought my own. Keep it in the cup and nobody will know the difference."

"Thanks," I said. I grinned and licked the foam off my upper lip. Josh had caught me dumping perfectly good beer into a potted palm and for some reason didn't think I was a total loser. What was wrong with him? I took another sip of root beer and the bubbles tickled my nose. We stood looking at each other, not saying anything for a long moment.

Josh tipped his cup to mine like he was making a toast. All of a sudden he seemed a little nervous. He leaned in, and it was all I could do not to put my hand out to touch his damp hair. "I'm glad you changed your mind about coming tonight," he said.

I quickly glanced into his eyes and then down at the peeling vinyl floor. "Yeah, I got done early," I managed.

"Have you been here a long time?" He probably wondered if I'd seen him and Justine.

"Long enough," I answered, and got a puzzled look in response. Before he could say anything, a group of guys slid the glass door open and rolled into the kitchen.

"Dude! Good to see ya." Dylan Roberts shoved his way in between us and gave Josh one of those complicated guy handshakes that ends with bumping fists. He did something on the football team and proved that fact to everyone by wearing his football jersey every day of every season. His broad back was facing me and a bright green number seven was right in my face.

"Hey, Dylan," Josh said. He spun Dylan around so he was facing me. "You know Lucy. From school." He said it more like a statement than a question.

"Right," Dylan said, looking me up and down in the most nonsubtle way imaginable. "You were JV cheer for basketball."

"No, I—" Instead of finishing, I grabbed a plastic cup from the counter. "You know what? Vanessa's going to be looking for that beer." I didn't want to make Josh look like a weirdo for sitting in the kitchen talking to me the whole time. He'd done his good deed for the night and now I was going to let him off the hook.

Josh touched my shoulder as I headed for the patio door. "What's the rush?"

I looked back at Dylan standing there with a couple of other football jocks. This was so not my crowd. It was like seeing famous people in real life, and having one of them actually talk to you. At least until they figured out you weren't one of them. "For one thing, I thought I'd leave you alone to hang out with your friends. And second, I don't want to keep Vanessa waiting."

"Vanessa's fine," Josh said. He indicated outside with his chin. "Look. She already got somebody else to get her another beer."

Through the glare of the light outside, I could see Vanessa talking to an older guy, flashing her teeth and tossing her hair. Sure enough, she had another blue cup of beer in her hand.

"And I can always spend a night sitting in somebody's kitchen talking to those idiots." He lowered his voice. "It's not every day I can spend some time talking to you."

It sounded like a line, and I had to look into his eyes to see if he was telling the truth. He was staring straight at me and not even smiling a little.

"Why?" It came out of my mouth before the censoring part of me had time to stop it.

Now Josh laughed. "Why?" he repeated.

"No, I didn't mean *why*, exactly," I started. "I just meant . . . I guess I don't know what I meant." This had started out so nice and I could feel myself blowing it. I took a deep breath and tried to calm down and not wreck it.

"No, no. It was a legitimate question," he said. He took

another sip from his cup, so that he had a tiny fleck of foam on his upper lip, and looked up at the ceiling. "Let's see . . . instead of spending the whole night listening to the guys detail the plays of every single winning game from last season, I could hang out with a pretty girl and find out why she's so mysterious." He looked at me from the corner of his eye. "Is that a good enough answer?"

"I suppose so," I said. "Except for the mysterious part. I'm about as unmysterious as you can get. And you see me all the time."

"I see you all the time. That's true. I see you in physics every day, where I've sat beside you for something like four months now and hardly heard you say a word. I see you at the café, where you always get a medium vanilla latte and barely even look at me when I hand it to you. You come and go, but I have no idea who you really are. Does that make sense?"

"What about Justine?"

"What about Justine?" he asked. "She's got nothing to do with me."

I glanced outside. "Yeah, but I saw you with her. When you were singing."

Josh flashed another smile. "That was just a show," he said. "It would have been perfect if you had been the one standing there instead of her."

More than anything, I wanted to believe him. I wanted to be able to look into his eyes and trust that what he was saying was the truth. But the truth was sometimes difficult to come by.

The sliding door opened and Kaylie walked into the kitchen. "I've been looking all over for you," she said, but she didn't sound mad. "You two just ran off together and never came back." She grinned at me and raised her eyebrows at Josh. Subtlety was a skill she was going to have to work on.

I straightened up and took a tiny step away from Josh. "Yeah, sorry. Josh just wanted to get something out of the fridge, so I came in here to help and—"

Kaylie waved her hand in the air. "It's fine. I'm not your mother. Anyway, Steve told us about this other party over on Hillside, and Vanessa wants to take off."

"No problem." I took a last swig of my root beer and put the cup down on the counter. "I'm coming."

Josh put his cup down next to mine. "I can't go for a while because I have to play another set. The provisional on my license just ended, so I could, uh, give you a ride home if you're not ready to leave," he said.

Part of me was thrilled, but more of me was terrified. Kaylie was like my lifeline in a foreign country, and it was scary to let her go. "No, really," I said. "It's fine. I'll just—"

"Great idea," Kaylie said. She turned to me and opened her eyes wide. "We're bringing a bunch of other people with us so the van's getting a little crowded, anyway."

I looked at Josh and he smiled, like I would be the one doing him a favor. If this night was going to count, I was going to have to take a chance. I could always get home on my own in time for my life to completely fall apart.

"Okay." I smiled back at him. "You really don't care?" I asked Kaylie.

She leaned in and gave me a quick hug. "Don't do anything I wouldn't do," she whispered in my ear, and with a smirk, she was gone.

I felt unmoored as the only person I really knew vanished into the crowd. Josh brushed my hand with the back of his, and I noticed, not for the first time, how strong his fingers were.

"You look like you could use another drink," he said, and grabbed my cup from the counter. I stood leaning against the sink as he poured more root beer into both of our cups. While he was busy, I allowed myself to enjoy his broad shoulders and easy smile. Not a bad way to spend the last normal night of my life, really.

"Are you spending the night at Kaylie's?" he asked.

"No," I said. "Not tonight."

"What time do you have to be home, then?" he asked. I followed his glance to a clock above the stove. 10:06.

I shrugged my shoulders. "Tonight? Tonight, it really doesn't matter." For once, I was telling the absolute truth.

chapter 18

2:30 a.m.

I glanced over my shoulder as the keys rattled in Josh's hand. "Are you sure it's okay?" I whispered.

He held the key ring up to the light of the lamppost on the corner. "Yeah, it's fine. Angie totally trusts me—that's why she made me assistant manager." He found a big square key and fit it in the lock. "Wait here one second," he said as he swung the door open and punched some numbers into the alarm system that hung by the front door.

I didn't know what time it was, but I figured it was way after midnight. I'd like to say that we spent the rest of the time at the party in meaningful conversation, but that would be a big fat lie. I spent the rest of the time at the party watching Josh as he played on the little stage out back. A couple of times during a song, he would look over, catch my eye, and smile at me. I stayed way in the back of the crowd rather than up in the front with the other drooling girls, but each time he smiled, a little thrill ran through me and I couldn't help smiling back.

The car ride here had been amazing. Once it was just the

two of us, it was like the whole world dropped away. We sat in the car out in front of the party for what seemed like hours, talking until the windows were steaming and it looked like we'd been doing a lot more. I had trouble regulating what I was saying about school and the future and not touching on the past. I wanted to live right here and right now—not tomorrow and not yesterday.

"There," Josh said as he pulled me through the front door. "If the alarm system went off, *then* she'd be pissed."

We stood in the darkened café. It was weird being in there with the lights off and nobody sitting at the tables or waiting in line to order a drink. The only light came from above the sink in back of the counter.

"This thing takes forever to heat up," Josh said, flicking buttons on the espresso machine. "You really don't have to be home?"

I shook my head and grinned. "Nope. Not tonight."

"Your mom must be really cool," he said. "Mine gets mad if I'm out past one, even during vacation."

"Let's just say my curfew isn't high on her priority list right now," I said. My mind flashed quickly to the sheet-wrapped figure in the hallway.

"Is your dad around?"

I just shook my head. I really didn't want to talk about me.

Josh was fiddling with stuff behind the counter. "My mom is on husband number three, and I think they get higher on the asshole scale every time."

"And you don't want to go live with your dad?"

He pulled a carton of milk out of the fridge. "Don't really know him. He took off when I was a baby. Last time I heard, he was living in New York, but that was a long time ago. Besides, I like it here. I figure I've got less than two years before I'm out of here, and I can put up with anything until then." For some reason, it made more sense when he said it.

"Do you know where you want to go to school?" I loved picking up little pieces of his life and putting them together to make the picture whole.

"I was thinking about Cal, but it's so close, you know? Mom is trying to get me to go someplace a little farther away, like UCLA or maybe Santa Barbara. Sometimes I think she's trying to get rid of me completely."

I laughed a little. I always wanted to go someplace as far away as possible. I was thinking about the East Coast, maybe Boston. I'd go farther than that, but you run out of country someplace around New York.

"Come here, you've got to take a whiff of this." Josh lifted the lid off a big gray garbage can that was sitting behind the counter.

My heart skipped a beat, and I could feel a shiver of fear run through my body as I stared at him with the garbage can lid in his hand. He knew. All this time and he was just setting me up for this moment. This whole thing *was* too good to be true. "Why?" I asked warily. I looked around, half expecting Justine and Cara to jump out from behind the counter pointing at Garbage Girl.

Josh laughed. "Stop asking so many questions and come over here. I promise you, this is one of the best smells in the world."

"Are you making fun of me?" I asked. I could feel my throat closing up, and the last thing I wanted to do was cry in front of him. I took a step back toward the door.

"No," he said, a look of concern crossing his face. "Why would I make fun of you? I just wanted to show you these." He reached into the can and pulled out a handful of shiny black coffee beans.

Relief flooded my body. I took a step forward and immediately the strongest, thickest coffee smell I'd ever imagined filled the air around me. The plastic can was filled almost to the rim with beans.

Josh laughed and took a deep breath. He stuck his face down close to the beans and inhaled again. "Oh my God, I love that smell. Sometimes when I have to work really early, I just come in here and stick my head in the can and breathe for a few minutes. I swear, you can almost get a buzz going off the smell alone." He took a scoop of the beans and put them in a big red machine. "Now, what can I get for you, miss?"

"What do you mean?"

"I mean, what would you like? Anything. On the house. If we're going to stay up late, we're going to need some assistance."

"I thought you had to be back by one o'clock," I said. "That was probably a long time ago."

"I said they get mad if I'm not home by one o'clock," he said. "I didn't say that I always do as I'm told. I'm working the early shift tomorrow, but I'm not about to abandon a girl with no curfew by going home on time."

"Well, thanks for risking it," I said.

"So, what'll it be?" he asked. "Medium vanilla latte, or would you like to go for something completely different?"

"Something completely different sounds exactly like what I need right now," I said. I leaned on the countertop and watched him work.

"So glad to hear you say that, Lucy Lu," he said. He turned on the red machine, and the noise of the grinding beans filled the empty space.

The last bit of my coffee was lukewarm as I tipped it out of the bottom of the paper cup. "That was awesome," I said. "What do you call it?"

"It's not on the menu," he said. "It has a little of this and a little of that, and I only make it for very special customers."

"So what do I have to do to get you to make it again?"

"All you have to do is show up," he said. "I'll call it the Lucy Special. But you can only have it made by me. If you go to any other coffee guys, you will definitely not get what you want." He tried to hide his grin by downing the last of his drink. "Hey, all we've been talking about is me—what about you?"

I shrugged. "What about me?" He was dangerously easy to talk to.

"Well, I know that you've seen every Johnny Depp movie ever made and that you like Shel Silverstein." I blushed, not expecting him to remember back that far. "Let's see—you live with your mom, who is religious but very cool with the curfews. Does your dad live around here?"

"No," I said. "He lives in Michigan with the new family." I couldn't believe all of this was sliding out of my mouth. It took months for me to tell Kaylie this much.

"That's a drag," Josh said. "Your mom never got married again?"

"Nope. She didn't . . . she doesn't even date or anything. Not since Dad left." I realized too late that I was already thinking of her in the past tense. Josh didn't seem to notice.

"You're lucky," he said. "My mom was never a good single person, which is why she makes such horrible choices. She's cool now, but before this last husband, she was drinking pretty heavy. I used to wake up in the morning and find her passed out on the couch from the night before, a couple of empty wine bottles on the floor."

It was hard to picture perfect Josh Lee coming from a broken home with an alcoholic mother. It didn't seem to bother him that much, though, and he talked about it like he was talking about what his mom did for work. Casually. Like it had nothing to do with him.

"Is that why you don't drink?" I asked.

"No. I wasn't drinking because I'm driving tonight. My mom got a DUI a few years ago and almost killed someone in an accident. It was a mess to undo—it still isn't all the way taken care of. I don't need that kind of trouble."

I smiled at him. "Is that the big family secret?"

Josh shook his head. "Not much of a secret," he said. "Not sure who knows, but it doesn't bother me. Just because she screwed up doesn't make it my problem."

I couldn't believe that it really wouldn't bother him that much. "Didn't you worry what people were going to say about her? About all of you?"

"They probably didn't say anything worse than I did at the time." He thought for a minute. "I guess at first I was pretty pissed off and embarrassed by the whole thing. Luckily, nobody ever saw her totally messed up, except for us. When she had the accident, it sort of blew the whole thing wide open, so we couldn't hide it anymore. It must have been before you started at our school, or believe me, you would have heard about it."

Josh looked at me from under a strand of dark, shining hair. "The funny thing is, it was almost a relief in a way. We were all forced to deal with it, instead of pretending everything was okay. She even met this husband at AA. He's a lot of things, but at least he's not a drunk."

I swallowed hard, thinking about what he'd said. Despite what everyone always said about "getting it all off your chest," I didn't buy it. Maybe someone could forgive an addiction, but nobody was going to understand how we lived under a mountain of garbage for so long. It was different. It made *us* too different.

"Are you the youngest?" I asked, wanting to absorb every scrap of information I could gather about him.

"Nope," he said. "Oldest. My brother's in eighth grade." He banged his hands on the table. "See, we're back to talking about me again. I think we need a little distraction." He grabbed my hand and pulled me up from the table where we were sitting. "Come with me."

I couldn't concentrate on where we were going because all of my attention was focused on where our skin was touching. He didn't let go, even when we were already standing up.

We walked through the dimly lit kitchen area to a large walk-in freezer on the back wall. Josh lifted the latch and pulled the door open, so a huge draft of cold air blasted us in the face.

"In there?" I asked.

"Just for a second," he said. "You still have your jacket on—you'll be fine."

I'd totally forgotten about my jacket and Teddy B., who was still stuffed in the bottom. I pulled it tighter around me and felt his softness cling to my side.

"Are you going to trust me this time?" Josh asked.

"Do I have a choice?"

"Of course you do," he said. "Hold out your hands." He handed me a white box and grabbed a silver canister. "Let's go back out front. It really is freezing in here."

Josh put the white box on the dark granite counter and opened it. It was full of small yellow cakes covered in chocolate. "Madeleines," he said. "Chocolate-covered madeleines." He handed me one of the shell-shaped cakes and shook the canister. Tipping it upside down, he made a perfect cloud on top. "Made even better with whipped cream."

I bit into the cake. It was cold and sweet and chocolaty— perfect after a hot cup of coffee. "Oh my God," I said. "This is awesome."

Josh jumped up and sat on the counter. I jumped up beside him.

"Tilt your head back," he said.

I did, and he squirted whipped cream right into my mouth. Laughing, I tried to shove it all in without making a huge mess, but I was sure I looked like a rabid dog. Josh tilted his head back and filled his mouth with whipped cream too. I watched him, suddenly conscious that we were alone in this dark, warm space.

"Come here." He smiled at me. "You have whipped cream on your nose." He leaned in and wiped the tip of my nose with his finger. Our heads were so close they were almost touching, and for once in my life I knew exactly what was going to happen next.

Josh tasted like whipped cream and chocolate and something else spicy and mysterious. Our lips touched tentatively at first, testing to see if we would pull away and then adding more pressure as neither of us did. Without saying a word, Josh jumped down from the counter and stood in front of me so he could reach up and run his fingers through my hair. For just a second, the sensation of his fingertips on my scalp was the only thing in the universe, and I had to open my eyes to regain my balance and sense of reality.

I reached out with my legs and wrapped them around his waist, pulling him closer to me as we explored each other's lips. Tracing his ear with the tip of my finger, I could feel him shake against my body.

After a few minutes, Josh pulled away just slightly and took my face in his hands. "You have no idea how long I've wanted to do that," he said, sounding a little out of breath. He traced my bottom lip with his finger and then leaned in to kiss the corner of my mouth. "You've got the most beautiful lips, Lucy Lu."

I laughed. I'd never thought of my lips as beautiful before— too big for my face, maybe, but hardly beautiful. This moment was so perfect I didn't want to say anything. I just pulled him close to me again and buried my face in the side of his neck, inhaling his scent so I would remember it forever. I felt so safe here in the dark of the café. Right here and right now, I could be the mysterious girl that Josh liked with the beautiful lips and no curfew.

As I leaned into him, I could feel Teddy B. bunched up under my jacket. I jumped down from the counter to face Josh, keeping one hand on my side so Teddy B. wouldn't slip out. I could explain away a lot of things, but having a homemade teddy bear under my jacket would really be pushing it.

I'm tall, but Josh had a good three inches on me as we stood facing each other in the dark. I eased my hands up his shirt and felt his back muscles moving under his warm skin. We were swaying slightly, like we were dancing to music only we could hear. I wanted to stay here and do this very same thing every day for the next hundred years.

"Can we do this again?" Josh said, like he was reading my mind. He put both arms around my back and kissed me behind one ear.

The sensation was so strong that I pulled back slightly. "Which part?" I asked.

"All of it," he answered. "I have to work until noon—will you meet me after?"

I started to say yes, and then the reality of what would be happening by noon hit me. By then, Sara would have found out what had happened to Mom, and the police would have been there for hours. Probably they would still be trying to get her out of that mess—amid curious neighbors and television crews who would want to document the process for the late news. By noon tomorrow, I'd be Garbage Girl again, for sure, and I'd lose all of this . . . all of him.

Josh pulled back so he could see my face. "Is that a yes, or a no?" he asked. To his credit, he looked genuinely worried.

"I really want to," I whispered. Even in the dim light, his face blurred as tears sprung into my eyes. I wanted it to be yes with all my heart. But I knew that by noon tomorrow it would be no. Josh reached up and tucked a piece of hair behind my ear and smiled at me, his dimples flashing and the warmth in his eyes making me feel safe and protected. I tried to make this one of those moments you can go back to forever—the feel of his skin under the palm of my hand, the throb of his heart beating at the base of his neck. I inhaled again to try to imprint his scent on my memory, but remembering these things was going to make them even harder to lose.

I tried to stay focused, but the image of the crowds in front of my house wouldn't go away. I wondered if Josh would be there too—gaping through the open door at the piles of filth that would always be a part of me. Even a guy like him wouldn't be able to get over my big secret. I didn't know if I could stand to see the look of disgust in his eyes and know that I'd lost the safety of his arms forever.

A digital clock above the espresso machine said 4:23. If I could just be me, alone, without the weight of Mom and the house hanging around my neck and pulling me down, everything would be perfect. In the movies, this would be the scene where the screen would fade to black—the house would disappear, leaving me untouched and able to face my future with Josh. If only this were one of those movies.

I traced my finger along his jawline, losing everything but the sensation of his body as it pressed against mine in the dark. The ache in my heart was so heavy my breath came in short, quiet gasps. Josh planted his hands firmly on my hips, his lips reaching for mine again, and I began to melt into the moment, the final moments of the last normal night of my life. If only the house *would* disappear—vaporize into the night until there was nothing left but Teddy B. in my jacket and my memories locked safely away where nobody would ever see. I'd gladly give up every single thing in that house, every ticket stub and handmade quilt, to be a regular girl with a best friend who really cared, and this boy whose touch left me speechless.

I pulled back from Josh's arms as the image hit me. I'd watched it a million times, but never thought of it as the answer until now. It was perfect. There was a way to save us all, but I had to work fast.

Josh's fingers were interlaced with mine as I stepped backward. "I have to go," I said. I let go and zipped my jacket up tighter.

He grabbed my hand and kissed my palm. "Are you sure? I have to be back here at seven, so I was thinking we could just hang out until then. I don't care about losing a little sleep."

Turning around, I kissed him hard on the mouth. He didn't know it then, but it was a promise. Maybe someday I could tell him what really went on tonight. Someday after. Right now, I had to keep this version of Lucy real for him and for me. "I'm sure."

I waited nervously while he put everything back and turned off the light. Now that I had it all figured out I didn't want to waste any time. His car was freezing, and I huddled in the front seat blowing on my hands while he warmed it up.

"I live just around the corner," I said, pointing up ahead.

He glanced at me while he drove. "I know where you live, Lucy Lu."

"You do?"

"Yep," he said, and grinned.

We kissed for another minute parked in front of the house. "I'll walk you to the door," Josh said, unbuckling his seat belt.

"No, really," I said quickly. "It's fine. You stay here—it's freezing outside."

"I'm not cold," he said, and reached over to kiss me again. It was going to be so hard to climb out of the car and walk away. I untangled myself from his arms and opened the door. I had to stay focused and not lose my nerve.

"Later? After work, okay—meet me there?" he asked. "I'll take you to lunch at the Paradise."

I nodded, kissed him one last time, and turned to walk quickly up the front steps. I had never felt so good and so bad at the same time. As I reached the door, I could hear his car idling, but I didn't turn around. I didn't want him to see the tears that had started rolling down my face. I didn't have time for tears once I got inside. If I wanted any more nights like this, I had no other choice.

4:45 a.m.

I pushed the front door open gently and stuck my head around into the hallway. I don't know what I expected to see, but it looked just the same as when I'd left.

I picked my way through the dining room to the back hallway. The light from the kitchen shone just enough to see the lumpy sheet. I looked at Mom lying there and tried not to let the lonely, helpless feelings wind around my body again. There was only one way to fix this—and standing here feeling sorry for myself wasn't going to make it happen. I just hoped it would work like it did in the movies.

As I dragged the space heater from my room, I could hear a faint beeping sound from far away. I followed the sound, walking back toward the front door. It was coming from somewhere near Mom's chair. As soon as I saw my bag on the floor, I realized what it was. My phone was ringing. At four something in the morning, my phone was ringing. As soon as the beeping stopped, I flipped open the phone and saw that I'd gotten seventeen text messages from Kaylie since I'd been out, and one from

Josh. The last one. *Sleep tite. J.* I stared at the text, imagining him on the other end of this phone, the light from his cell shining on his skin in the dark. The longing was a physical ache in my chest, but I shut the phone and set it on the chair. Everything good would have to wait.

I crossed to the dining room and stuck my head out the window, inhaling the sharp, cold air. The clouds had vanished overnight, leaving a surprising number of stars twinkling in the space between our roof and the trees that separated our yard from the Rajs'. There was about half of a football field between our house and theirs, which was perfect.

I wasn't even nervous as I made my way back toward my room. Now that I knew what I had to do, it seemed almost easy. I wouldn't be able to explain why I was in jeans in the middle of the night, though, so I had to change into the T-shirt and sweats that I usually slept in.

As I passed the corner to Mom's room, I spotted those scabby suede slippers sticking forlornly out of the sheet. It would only take a minute, I told myself. For some reason it felt like the right thing to do. I inched my way back toward the front of the house and found the box where I'd left it yesterday. Tearing through the tissue paper, I pulled out the new slippers, tucking them under my right arm as I made my way back through the kitchen. I knelt down at her feet and gently pulled the old, worn slippers off, trying not to look at her yellow toenails or her mottled bone white skin while I slipped the new ones on. As I stood up, I squeezed the right foot with my hand. It was as close to a good-bye as I was going to get. I had to keep telling myself it was better this way. I had to believe it.

Setting her old slippers down on my bed, I took a long look

around my room. I'd never lived anywhere else, and I knew every crack in the ceiling and worn spot in the carpet. As much as I couldn't wait to get out of here, I was going to miss it. This was where Mom taught me to sew and where once upon a time we all lived together as a family. I reminded myself that this was also where I lived without a door to my room or hot water for years. I ran my hand over the quilt on my bed and looked at the lunchbox that held my tickets. If I started to think about all the things I wanted to save, I'd never get it done. I had to get started.

I changed into Phil's old AC/DC concert shirt and gray sweatpants as fast as I could because it was so freezing in here. Grabbing the stinky slippers off the bed, I stood in the doorway and took one last look around. Everything else had to stay. Teddy B. was in a heap on the floor with my jacket, and I felt a pang in my chest. I hadn't seen him for years, but I felt like he was one link to the past that I wasn't ready to give up. I grabbed him and stuck him in the waistband of my sweats. I'd stash him some-place safe until it was all over and he could be with me again.

I took a deep breath and turned toward the door. Time to start my after.

chapter 20

5:25 a.m.

Starting the fire was harder than I thought it would be. When Johnny Depp and his sisters burned their house down in *What's Eating Gilbert Grape*, they took what they wanted out of the house and then poured gasoline over everything else. Gasoline wasn't part of my plan—I had to use the natural layout of the house to make this place burn beyond recognition while making it look like an accident. And I couldn't take anything with me.

I plugged the space heater into the extension cord by Mom's chair, and to my surprise, it started whirring without even needing a smack to get it started. As soon as the coil inside was glowing orange, I placed the heater next to a stack of newspapers and kicked it over just enough so that it was pressed against the flammable pile. I stood back and waited for the flames to burst from the heater and blaze up the wall.

Nothing happened.

I'd always thought that the smallest thing would burn this place down to the ground. We were always worried that a spark from an electrical short or a stove malfunction would send the place up in flames in seconds. Apparently it took a little more effort. I pushed the heater deeper into the stack and stood back, watching for the smallest wisp of smoke to signal success.

I smelled it before I saw it—that faint campfire smell when something starts to burn. Just as the smell registered in my brain, there was a brief burst of smoke before the edge of one of the papers caught fire.

It didn't roar and it didn't jump to life—the fire unfolded purposefully before my eyes as if it were an animal that was slowly coming out of hiding, creeping forward and waiting to see if I was going to chase it back into its cave.

I'd been concentrating so hard on starting the fire that once it caught I wasn't sure exactly what to do. It had to be going really strong before I went for help, so I just watched the flames creep up the stack of newspapers as if they were the yule log we always watched on TV on Christmas mornings. I could see it, I could smell it, and eventually, I could feel the heat from it, but it was like it didn't really have anything to do with me.

The smoke was starting to gather and swirl at the ceiling as I stepped back into the dining room. It invaded my nostrils and I tried to take short shallow breaths so that it wouldn't go deeper. I crouched down a little where the air was clearer and hoped that I could still get out easily.

In a fairly short time, the fire knew it was beyond any decision I could make and was quickly spreading in this part of the house. A little zing of panic raced through me as I realized I'd actually done it—the house was really on fire and nothing I could do now would stop it.

The front door was totally blocked by the flames that had

streaked across the living room, up the curtains, and were now curling around themselves where the walls met the ceiling. Squinting against the heat and smoke, I stood in the dining room at the edge of the flames, like I was at a bonfire on the beach. I ran my hand over the bottoms of Mom's old slippers, worn smooth by years of trudging through the pathways of our house. Once they were new and full of promise, but after Mom got through with them, they were beyond repair. One by one I tossed them into the fire like an offering.

The smoke was rolling across the ceiling toward the open dining room window, so I followed it, climbing onto the ledge and landing in the pile of garbage bags below with barely a sound. I crawled out of the pile, my leg momentarily sinking between some of the bags until I pulled it free, the plastic cold and damp against my skin.

I stood outside under the tall, bare trees, watching through the open window as the fire coursed through the living room and raced down the hall. Fingers of flames started to lick the walls of the dining room, and I felt a pang of regret as they reached my neat, four-high stack of green bins. Soon they'd reach Grandma's trunk and devour all of the evidence that Mom was once something special. Petey's cage would be next, followed by TJ's set of encyclopedias.

When the heat grew too intense and I could hear windows popping in the back of the house, I knew it was over. I backed away from the flames, through the line of trees, and then ran across the wide expanse of dewy, well-tended grass to the Rajs' front porch. I could see the orange glow at the back of our house near Mom's bedroom and knew that the fire's appetite was total.

I remember banging on the front door and the panic around me as the fire department was called, frantic shouts, and nodding numbly when they asked if Mom was still inside, the fire now spewing from every available orifice in the house, preventing even the bravest attempt at rescue.

A blanket appeared over my shoulders, and as I pulled it around me, my fingers felt the lump of Teddy B. where he was still curled up safe and warm inside the waistband of my pants. I'd meant to hide him somewhere, but I'd forgotten. The edge of the blanket was scratchy, and I vaguely wondered why people were always wrapped in blankets at the scene of a tragedy. Whether it was loved ones waiting on shore for news of someone lost at sea or surveying a house that had been demolished in a hurricane, every photo always had the survivors wrapped in a blanket, even if it wasn't particularly cold outside. There was something in the gesture of having a blanket wrapped around you that signaled that you were safe and that someone cared enough to make sure you were wrapped up and warm.

I was just a normal girl watching her entire life burn to the ground, hoping that she'd never have to explain the feeling of relief that was rising from the pit of her stomach and threatening to lift her into the air. As I heard the sharp sound of sirens growing louder in the distance, I pulled the blanket tighter around me, safe in my cocoon.

Someone handed me a tissue, and I looked at it blankly until I realized my face was wet and tears were beading on the edge of the blanket I was wrapped in. I stood for a minute, watching the arcs of water from the fire trucks that beat down on the remains of my life. Mom was gone, and there would be no house to fix up and live in happily ever after. The after that I'd pictured was going to be a lot different than I'd thought it would be. But that wasn't necessarily a bad thing.

The crowd of people around me shifted, and I was suddenly enveloped in a warm, wool jacket that smelled of soap and perfume. "Oh my God!" Kaylie's mom released me long enough to look me over. "I was on my way to work when I saw the fire. Lucy, honey, are you all right?"

I nodded slowly, watching the flames climb higher and higher. Mrs. Raj leaned over and whispered something in her ear, and I watched Kaylie's mom's eyes fill with tears. She put her arm around me and sniffed, shaking the sadness off and standing up straighter. "Whatever you need," she said. "We're here for you. I'll stay here with you as long as you like, and then we're going straight home to find you some warm clothes."

Leaning into her shoulder, I felt her strength as she propped me up. I turned away from the fire then, not because I couldn't stand to watch it anymore, but because I was done with it.

In the distance, over the hills, a pink, streaky, hopeful glow was emerging that rivaled the hot angry glow behind me. The skeletal trees pulsed with the red beat of the flashing lights, and neighbors gathered on their driveways, hands to their mouths in disbelief. As I looked at individual faces, I saw concern, not disgust, and wondered how different it would have been just a few hours from now if it were news camera crews instead of fire trucks in front of our house.

Mom had made the mess, and I was the only one left who could clean it up. For sixteen years, I'd gone along with it all, until I finally took control. I kept the secrets safe.

acknowledgments

From first inspiration to the book you hold in your hands, it took a lot of people to make it a reality. It would just be a file on a laptop without my agent, Erin Murphy, who read it, believed in it, and then made it happen. Thanks to my editor, Mary Kate Castellani, whose gentle nudges resulted in big improvements, and to everyone at Walker who supported this concept from the start. Big thanks go to my critique partners who read it and steered me in the right direction: Natalie Lorenzi, Ammi-Joan Paquette, Julie Phillips, Kip Wilson, Lindsey Levitt, Maurene Hinds, Shelley Seeley, and Angela Cerrito. I'm grateful to Cassandra Whetstone, who sat up late into the night tossing ideas around and who gave me one of Lucy's best lines. Writer-mentor Karen English should have laughed at my first feeble writing attempts, but her encouragement kept me going.

This book wouldn't exist without my personal support system. My boys are the best—Bayo, Jaron, and Taemon dutifully ignored me when my characters carried on conversations out loud and supported me despite my constant distraction. Mom, Joe, Dad, Sue, Jessica, and Wendy collectively gave me the tools I needed to find my voice. Jessica Romero and Barbara Stewart screamed when the news was good and fed me chocolate when the news was bad. The biggest piece always came from Karen Ryan, my blindly supportive friend and very own personal publicist.

Finally, this book is for every child who grew up with a shameful secret. Donna Austin, Elizabeth Nelson, and Tracy Schroeder shared scraps of their lives and weren't afraid to tell me when I was getting it wrong. If you or someone you know is affected by compulsive hoarding, seek help—this psychological disorder touches millions of people worldwide, and you are not alone. The website www.childrenofhoarders.com is a great resource for ideas and a supportive community of people who have shared the experience and truly understand.

DIRTY
LITTLE
SECRETS

Reading Group Guide

1. Lucy's life is difficult and dangerous because of her mother's hoarding. Do you think her mother is selfish or does she have a mental disorder? Do you think her mother's behavior qualifies as abuse?

2. Do you watch any of the hoarding shows on television? Have you ever seen things in the shows that are also in the book? What does this say about how different hoarders behave?

3. Lucy feels that she can't tell anyone about her mother's hoarding problem. Could she have confided in Kaylie? Josh? What do you think would have happened if she'd told someone?

4. Sara and Phil react to their mother's problem in different ways; why do you think that is? Are there any indications in the story that hoarding might be a hereditary problem?

5. Lucy likes to save certain things, like tickets from movies or the circus. Do you think she could grow up to develop hoarding issues?

6. To the outside world, Lucy's mom is a perfectly normal person who works as a nurse. Many people with a hoarding disorder are in nurturing fields such as teaching or nursing—why do you think that is?

7. Lucy's mother can't throw anything away. Is there a pattern to the things that she saves? Do they say anything about who she is as a person?

8. Lucy has always kept people at a distance. Why does she choose to let Kaylie and Josh into her life, even a little bit?

9. Lucy's reaction to her mother's death isn't what you expect. Why doesn't she call 911 right away? Do her actions make sense in her situation?

10. The author uses flashbacks to give us a glimpse into Lucy's entire life. Do they help you understand why she reacts the way she does? What is your favorite memory in the book?

11. Eight-year-old TJ is the one person that Lucy finally confides in and allows inside the house. Why do you think she picks him?

12. At the end of the book, Lucy chooses to take only one possession with her—Teddy B. What is so special about that choice? Does he symbolize anything for her?

13. Lucy's secret is that her mother is a hoarder, but people try to keep all sorts of things secret. What other secrets might someone go to great lengths to keep hidden?

14. Lucy makes a drastic decision about how to fix her problem. Do you think she makes the right choice? What would you do if you were in her situation?

15. The end of the book leaves many questions unanswered— what do you think happens next? Where will Lucy go to live? Are her secrets ever revealed? Will she be caught for her actions?

Past lives change all the rules
for life and love.

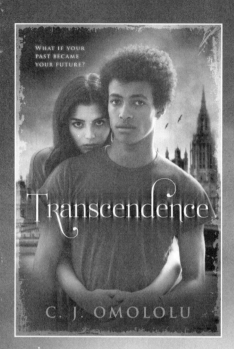

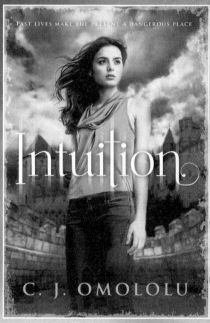

Don't miss C. J. Omololu's epic
reincarnation love stories . . .

C. J. Omololu didn't grow up in a hoarded home, but she has seen what the disorder can do to a family through her research with the Children of Hoarders organization. *Dirty Little Secrets* is her first novel. She lives in Northern California with her husband and two sons.

www.cjomololu.com

LOOKING FOR ANOTHER DARK AND COMPELLING READ?

Don't miss these extraordinary novels about teens dealing with some tough stuff.

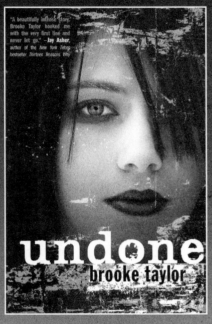

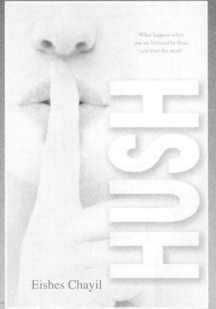